OUT-DWELLER

Glimmer Vale Chronicles #2

MICHAEL KINGSWOOD

Copyright © 2013 by Michael Kingswood

Cover Art by crisshasart, contracted through fiverr.com

Interior Art by Jared Blando

ISBN 13: 978-0998068442

Parties interested in licensing rights to this property, should contact publisher@ssnstorytelling.com

CONTENTS

ABOUT THIS BOOK

A series of brutal murders puts constables Raedrick Baletier and Julian Hinderbrook on the trail of a killer.

With Lydelton's populace growing increasingly uneasy and few leads to follow, they must move quickly to find the culprit and bring his reign of terror to an end.

But they are not the only ones who are hunting, and some foes require more than just skill at arms to defeat.

Out-Dweller is the second book of the Glimmer Vale Chronicles, a sword and sorcery mystery set in a world of valor and magic.

Enjoy the book! After you're done, please come to Michael's website and sign up for his mailing list at www.michaelkingswood.com/newsletter-signup/. Guaranteed to be spam free, he uses it to announce new releases and special promotions for his fans.

MAP OF GLIMMER VALE

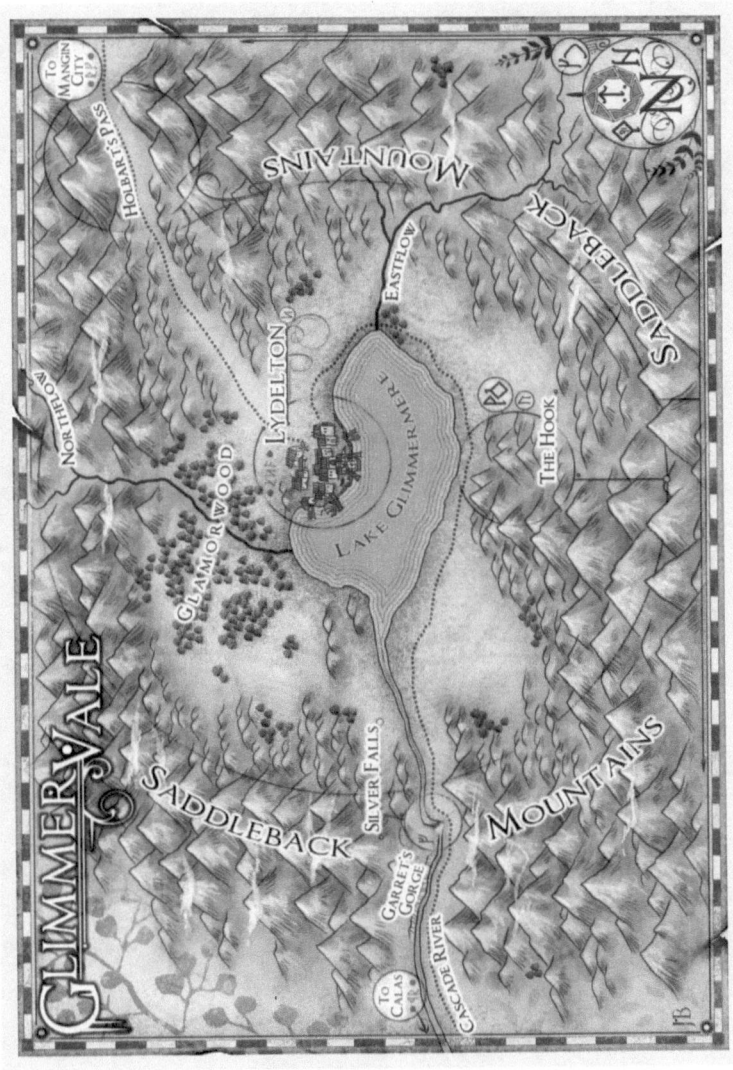

FRESH KILL

B aelin unstrung his bow and shoved it over his right shoulder, under the strap of his backpack, then crouched down and gathered the spoils of the day's hunt. It had taken a while to dress out the buck and he would lose the light soon; it was well past time to get back home. Ilsa would begin to worry if he tarried too much longer, to say nothing of the scolding she would unleash if he caused dinner to grow cold.

He smiled at the contradiction in her possible reactions - and he had seen them both before. But then that was the essence of woman was it not? Contradiction.

The buck was heavier than it looked, and it took a moment to get it settled over his left shoulder and balanced well. Baelin adjusted his brown hunting cloak a bit so that it settled better over himself; summer was coming to a close, and the evening's chill had grown bitter over the last week. Then he set off down the hill toward town.

The northern slopes of the mountains surrounding Glimmer Vale were covered in dense evergreens and he had to weave his way through a seeming maze of tree trunks as he made his way back toward Lake Glimmermere and Lydelton. Many a man with limited experience had gotten lost in these woods, called the

Glamorwood by the locals. Some of the more gullible townsfolk told tall tales of spirits living amongst the trees. So with the exception of logging expeditions that never went in further than the edges of the forest and outdoorsmen like Baelin, most people from Lydelton and the town's surrounds did not venture here.

Which suited Baelin just fine. Most people were not worth dealing with, and the fewer who came here the more likely he was to be able to enjoy the woods in peace.

And it made venison more rare in town, which meant he could charge more for his take.

Baelin's smile grew a bit more broad at that thought.

The shadows were growing long now as the sun made its way to its resting place in the east, below the ridges of the Saddleback Mountains. Off to the right, a Night Thrush called out, breaking the silence with its ululating chirp. Baelin quirked an eyebrow; it was a bit early to hear that particular breed up and about, but the early bird gets the worm, or something.

He descended further, moving carefully to avoid tripping in the elongating shadows. After about a quarter of an hour he stopped for a moment. The buck was heavy. That was good, made for more meat. But it was growing uncomfortable carrying it as he was; the muscles in his left shoulder were beginning to shout in protest and he felt a cramp coming on.

Grumbling to himself, Baelin rolled his right shoulder and shoved the bow further down. Then with a huff he shifted the buck over to his right and rebalanced himself before heading off again.

A few paces later, a snort from off to his left stopped Baelin in his tracks. What was that?

He turned his head, peering around carefully and trying to ignore the sudden whisper of alarm that began to take shape within him. He had never heard a sound like that out here before, and he had tracked or hunted just about everything that lived in these woods at one time or another.

The snort came again, a bit louder this time. With it came a strange odor that seeped into the normal scent of fallen pine needles like a bit of dye dropped into a cup of water. He almost had not noticed it was there at all, subtle as the new scent was. Sharp and tangy, with an unpleasant undertone, like something rotten.

Baelin scowled, that whisper becoming more like a person speaking in a normal tone of voice now. He shivered from a surge of adrenalin. Something was not right here.

He stood there for a long several moments, his free left hand resting on the grip of his long hunting knife, where it was sheathed on his hip. His left was not his best hand, but he was not completely inept with it. And right then the feel of the weapon in hand was all that mattered.

The odor grew stronger, and a branch snapped somewhere behind him. Baelin turned quickly. The buck slid off his shoulder and landed on the ground with a muffled thud, but he paid it no mind.

He squinted, trying to see what was out there, but the light was going fast, and here beneath the canopy of the trees it was already getting on toward twilight.

He saw nothing, but that was no comfort. *Something* was out there. Something foul.

Calm down. You're not some tenderfoot, out in the woods for the first time and scared of his own shadow. It's just a hog.

The thought was logical, but Baelin's instincts rejected it out of hand. No hog ever smelled like this.

He looked around for another minute or so, the strange odor growing steadily stronger the entire while, but still saw nothing. Neither was there any other sound besides the tree limbs stirring in the breeze and the pounding of his own heart.

It was nothing. He just stumbled a bit too close to the remains of some predator's kill.

And speaking of which, he had his own kill to take care of, and it was well past too late to be out in these woods.

Baelin crouched back down and maneuvered the buck back

onto his shoulder; his left this time. Straightening, he turned back toward town.

And came face to face with something right out of his nightmares.

His scream, loud and terrified, echoed through the woods for a long several seconds before it abruptly cut off in a strangled gurgle.

Then all was silent.

BREAKING FAST

J ulian spat the last of his teeth-cleaning solution into his little washbowl, then straightened and smirked at himself in the mirror. He had almost become civilized.

He took a moment to lace up his boots—brown leather, weathered and comfortable, that came almost to his knees —then he pinned his badge of office, a silver fist grasping a set of scales, onto the breast of his dark green tunic and strapped on his sword belt. A moment later he was out the door, ready to face another day as the hammer of justice.

Or, more likely, the solver of middling disputes.

As he pulled the door to his small flat shut behind him and locked up, Julian reflected that life as Constable of Lydelton was not quite what he thought it would be. Hardly surprising, considering how he and Raedrick came into the job. But still, he had expected a bit more excitement, more challenge.

In retrospect, he should have known better. Lydelton, though prosperous, was not a large town. When the merchant caravans were not in town—and they were few these days—only a few hundred people, maybe a thousand tops, lived in the town proper. That did not make for much in the way of crime, at least among the locals. The rest of the Vale held probably double that number, but they were spread around enough that Julian hardly ever interacted with them; for the most part they took care of matters that needed taking care of themselves, and resented having their business butted into.

So Julian's days mostly consisted of sitting in the Constable's Office and making sure the place was kept up, making a stroll or two around town and checking in on the various businesses and residents, and preparing the weekly report to Mayor Brimly.

Hardly the epitome of excitement. But then again, it could be worse. A lot worse. Julian had seen more than his fair share of action and, for lack of a better term, excitement in the Army, on the front lines. Though it was more like moments of sheer terror between weeks of absolute boredom and frivolous make-work. The quiet life here in Lydelton was quite an improvement from that.

A narrow set of stairs led from his flat's doorway to the ground floor below. Julian took them two at a time and emerged a moment later onto the street outside.

His flat rested on the second floor of a small building on Cannery Street, two blocks from both Main Street to his right and Lake Glimmermere, with its multitude of fishing docks, to his left. The first floor of his building was dominated by his landlord's canvas shop, which supplied sails and other gear to the fishermen on their boats. Master Feldmyn did a steady business from what Julian could see, which explained why he lived in a good-sized house on the west side of town instead of in the flat above his shop. And why the rent on the flat was so reasonable.

Or it could have been Julian's status as a genuine local hero that lowered the rate, but he doubted it.

Julian turned right toward Main Street, but took the first right and walked several blocks down until The Oarlock came into view. Two stories tall and impeccably kept up, the Inn had quickly become Julian's favorite supplier of drink, food, and company.

He wasted no time, but strode quickly up to the main entrance and stepped inside.

As always, it took a moment for his eyes to adjust to the relative gloom of The Oarlock's taproom. The windows were few, and draped, letting only a small amount of sunlight within. Instead, oil lamps on sconces around the room lent a dim, flickering glow to the place. When it got colder, they would be augmented by fires from the twin fireplaces in the corners to his right and left, but for now the fireplaces were empty, barren.

A long bar stretched along the length of the wall to his right. The remainder of the room was filled with tables, most of them unoccupied at this early hour. A staircase in the rear corner led up to the rooms on the second level, mostly unrented at this point unless Julian missed his guess; it had been some time since a caravan, or any travelers, had come through the Vale. A set of swinging double-doors at the rear led into the kitchens, and off in the rear right lay a less obtrusive doorway that led out to the lower level privy.

It almost felt like coming home.

Julian sidled up to the middle of the bar, where a woman of late middle years, dressed in a simple brown dress and a white apron, was wiping down the taps with a pristine white rag. He had never seen Molli ever use a dirty rag for that job; he supposed the dust was likely too scared to come anywhere near her bar, as much a neat nick as she was.

Molli flashed a warm smile at Julian as he settled down onto one of the stools lining the bar. "You're late," she said.

Julian snorted. "It's not yet 8 o'clock." He glanced aside, toward the mantel overtop the fireplace on the right, where a large wooden clock ticked away the day's hours. The Gods alone knew where Molli acquired the gold to afford something like that; she sure was not telling.

Molli shook her head in response, then pulled a plate that was covered by an off-white cloth napkin out from where it had been resting below the bar. She slid it across the polished wooden surface toward him. "This has been growing cold for ten minutes," she said, and quirked an eyebrow at him. "You're late."

Julian could only spread his hands helplessly and give her an abashed smile. There really was no other response; she had him cold.

Molli looked gravely at him for a few seconds, then chuckled and turned away, toward where a pitcher that was beading with condensation sat next to the taps. She grabbed a goblet from a shelf above the bar and filled the goblet with dark fluid from the pitcher, then set it next to the plate, along with a fork and knife. "Eat up."

"Yes, ma'am," Julian said, inclining his head in supplication.

He whipped the napkin off and revealed his breakfast: lightly fried fish bits, fresh caught from the lake of course, alongside finely chopped and baked potatoes and a hard-fried egg. Combined with the cold-brewed tea in the goblet, it was everything his belly needed to be happy for a good long time.

Julian considered, for the hundredth time, that it would be better to eat slowly, savor every morsel. Somewhere in the back of his head, he heard his mother's voice saying that was more healthy. Or something. But in the end, the rumbling of his stomach won out, and in the space of just a few minutes half the food on his plate was gone. It was beyond delicious, as always. It pained him for a second that so little remained to eat. And then he set to again.

Molli spoke again at some point, but he missed what she said, so engrossed was he in the joy of breakfast well crafted.

"Eh?" Julian managed after swallowing.

Molli rolled her eyes. "I said, has Ilsa Rorickson come to see you?"

Julian raised an eyebrow and took a drink of tea to give himself time to think. Rorickson. Who was... Ah, the woodsman's wife. Her face came into Julian's mind: round, just past homely toward cute, not showing nearly the amount of care lines one would expect from a woman her age, with sharp green eyes and a narrow nose beneath light brown hair. He had only interacted with her and her husband a couple times in the months since he and Raedrick took over for the late Constable. They seemed decent enough, if a bit standoffish.

"Should she have?"

Molli pursed her lips slightly. "She was in here late last night, looking for Baelin. Caused a bit of a fuss."

Julian raised an eyebrow. "So?"

"Apparently he didn't come home last night. Ilsa all but accused Helena Winslow of helping her sister steal him away."

Oh brother. Another one of *those* problems. Julian sighed and dropped his fork onto his plate, the metallic clank making a fine counterpoint to the annoyance surging within him. "I'm not a bloody marriage counsellor," he muttered, scowling.

Molli smirked back at him. "Sure you are. Goes with that fancy pin you wear around." She gestured toward his badge of office.

Julian met her gaze levelly for a moment, then groaned and picked his fork back up. He went back to shoveling his breakfast into his mouth, the succulent flavors suddenly tasting a bit more bitter than normal.

It was going to be a bad day. He could see it already.

COMMUTE

The walk from The Oarlock to his and Raedrick's small Constabulary seemed to drag, though it was only a few blocks. Julian strongly suspected he would find Ilsa there, slinging accusations of her husband's infidelity, and he really did not want to deal with that. This was what passed for excitement these days, and for a moment Julian almost found himself wishing for some nice honest brigands to fight off.

He shoved that thought away, a half-remembered twinge of pain from his left thigh almost causing him to limp for a pace or two. They had been damn lucky, beating Isenholf's group of bandits. The fight could easily have gone the other way. And even though the town emerged victorious, several good men had paid with their lives, and many people's livelihoods had been harmed; some were only now beginning to recover from the episode, months later.

So no, the drudgery of playing wedding savior was much preferable to the alternative.

Julian emerged onto Main Street and smirked as his boots went from kicking up dust to clumping along on the well-laid flagstones of Lydelton's only paved street. Why they had not bothered with the other streets was beyond him, and Raedrick had never been able to properly explain it. Nor had anyone else in town, for that matter.

He turned right and strolled another block, nodding to a pair of men who were just starting up the day's business as they opened their leatherworking shop. A moment later, he paused as a gaggle of children burst out from another building. The group was ushered along by a pair of nearly identical older ladies, their grey hair done up in matching buns and their dresses matched to compliment each other's colors. That was on purpose, Julian was certain.

The group of youngsters giggled their way past him and the lady in the rear nodded her head politely to him. "Constable."

Julian grinned and made a little bow. "Good morning, Beverlee," he said brightly, earning a flash of a smile from her before she swept past.

Julian watched the procession maneuver down the street, then turn left toward the docks. Must be a lesson about the lake, or how boats work.

"Damn shame, that," a gruff voice said.

Julian turned toward the speaker, a short but powerfully built man in his early middle years. Grey flecked the black hair on his head, and he had a puckered scar over his left eyebrow. He wore a simple white shirt and brown pants, and carried a heavy leather apron slung over one shoulder that smelled of woodsmoke and metal. A blacksmith, evidently. Julian did not know him.

"What is?"

The smith nodded toward Beverlee, just before she disappeared around the corner. "Keep forgetting you're new around here. Them two were the loveliest lasses in town, once." He grunted. "Never married though; said they never wanted to. Just lived together and taught the kids, nothin' more."

Julian frowned. "Nothing wrong with teaching."

The smith snorted, casting a baleful look Julian's way. "'Course not. That's not the shame of it." He turned away, shaking his head, and stomped off down the street, continuing back on his way to work.

Julian watched him go. The man paused at the cross-street the ladies and children turned down. Julian could have sworn he looked down the street with longing in his eyes for a moment before moving on himself.

Julian stopped in front of his destination and paused, contemplating whether he really wanted to go in or not.

The building he shared with Raedrick was small, one story tall and constructed of pale-stained wood. A pair of hitching posts flanked the stairs leading up to the front porch, which ran the length of the building. The hitching posts were empty; hardly unusual, considering how few of the townfolk rode horses as part of their daily routine. Overall, the building had an official look to it that went beyond the simple sign reading "Constable" above the front door. Maybe it was the iron bars over the windows.

Might as well get to it. With a small sigh, Julian strode up the stairs and stepped inside.

The front room stretched the length of the building. A pair of desks faced each other on either side of the room; his on the left, Raedrick's on the right. A shelf with a number of books—city ordnances, the laws of the kingdom, local histories, that sort of thing—stood against the far wall, near the steel-barred door that led back into the cell block. A chest-high cabinet with a multitude of small drawers containing case files and the like stood on the other side of the cell block door. Behind Raedrick's desk was a rack of swords, behind Julian's a rack of bows and his favorite feature of their office: a small but very well constructed fireplace.

Raedrick was already at work, sitting behind his desk and reviewing some paperwork, when Julian walked in. As always, his friend wore his black hair tied into a short pony tail at the nape of his neck and was dressed well, in a dark blue shirt that was open at the collar.

Raedrick looked up as Julian entered and grinned. "You're late."

Julian rolled his eyes. "Everyone's been saying that today." He stomped over to his desk, unhooked his scabbard from his belt and leaned it against the wall, then sat down and kicked his feet up. "Hear about the fuss over at The Oarlock last night?"

Raedrick quirked up one eyebrow. "In gruesome detail."

Julian chuckled. No doubt Lani had left no detail out. She was Molli's daughter and worked the inn as well. She was also Raedrick's "friend", though Julian wondered how long they were going to keep up that charade rather than just come out and admit what everyone in town knew: they were sweet on each other. Disgustingly so.

"Wonder how long it'll take before she shows up here," Julian quipped, trying to sound amused rather than resigned about the situation.

Raedrick did not respond to Julian's attempt at frivolity. Leaning back in his chair, he ran one finger absently along the edge of his desk for a few seconds, frowning. Finally, he said, "From what I hear, it's not like Baelin to not return home as planned."

Julian gave him a level look. "All sorts of reasons why a man might have to spend the night out in the woods." Or, for that matter... "Or not in the woods."

Raedrick nodded, still frowning, but did not reply.

It took a lot longer for them to get company than Julian thought it would, but it was not Ilsa who came to see them.

Shortly after noon, the door to their office opened to admit a tall, lean man who was well along in years but still walked with the posture and vigor of youth despite the deep canyons lining his face. His hair was fully grey, with only a few wisps of its original black still showing, and hung loosely past his shoulders. He boasted a full beard of similar color that reached nearly to the collar of the leather jacket he wore in spite of the lingering late-summer heat. Like him, the jacket showed signs of great age. Also like him, that age did not seem to do anything except make the jacket better. It hung down to the man's thighs, covering up a patched set of clothes that looked made to blend in with the forest. He bore an unstrung bow in his left hand, and a quiver hung over his shoulder. A long hunting knife and knee-high boots that looked to be ridiculously comfortable completed an ensemble that screamed "woodsman" louder than a company of men shouting in unison.

The old man squinted at them from just inside the entranceway for a moment, then snorted. "You two're the lawmen 'round here." Julian was not sure whether it was a statement or a question.

Raedrick answered first. "We are. I'm Raedrick Baletier and that's Julian Hinderbrook." He stood from his desk and walked around it, extending his hand for a shake. "How can we help you?"

The old woodsman looked at Raedrick's extended hand as though uncertain what his intentions with it were, then shrugged and gestured toward the door. "Got something you want to take a look at, in the hills above town."

Julian and Raedrick exchanged glances. "What sort of some-thing, Master..." Julian left the sentence die away into a question.

The old man grunted. "Man got himself torn up. Ain't never seen nothing like it." He grimaced, as though talking about it was bringing up an unpleasant vision. For a moment, it almost looked like the man was going to be sick right there.

This was not good at all.

❧ 4 ❧

GLAMORWOOD

I t was not until they were almost out of town, following Main Street northwest toward the forest-covered hills beyond, that the old woodsman finally revealed his name. It took Raedrick finally straight-out asking, instead of the polite half-question Julian had tried in the office.

The old man squinted at Raedrick as though surprised for a heartbeat or two, then shrugged. "Name's Dewey." He left it at that, focusing his attention on the road ahead.

Julian exchanged glances with his friend, who shrugged and smiled slightly, clearly amused. Julian was inclined to agree. The old man was eccentric, for sure. But, looking at the signs of more decades than most men ever saw on Dewey's face, Julian figured he had earned the right.

They passed the last buildings on Main Street, and with them the road's paving stones. Just like that, Lydelton lay behind them and they were strolling through rolling grasslands that stretched on as far as Julian could see off to east. To the north and west, though, evergreen trees loomed a mile or so away. Even at the outskirts of the Glamorwood, the trees were tall and proud. Julian knew men went into the woods from time to time to harvest lumber, but they were either very careful about it or the forest grew back very efficiently; he could see no sign of logging's impact on the woods. Maybe they simply were not close enough to notice.

But as they drew nearer, the pristine look of the forest remained, and Julian was forced to conclude the logging men simply went elsewhere. It was a large forest, after all.

The road ended at the edge of the forest in front of a low building. Constructed of carefully placed stones that were held together with mortar, with a thatch roof that looked freshly changed-out, it looked as though it had stood in that place since the mountains had first come to be. A small sign hung next to the narrow wooden door that was set in the middle of the building's front wall. It read, "Ranger Station".

Julian blinked, surprised. "There are Rangers stationed here?" An icy shiver of concern raced down his spine as he waited for Dewey's reply. The Rangers were officials from the Kingdom. They would certainly have heard of Julian and Raedrick's status in town, and of their past. And they would certainly have reported it.

Perhaps this place was not to be home after all.

Glancing to his left, Julian saw a similar concern on his friend's face, though Raedrick hid it well enough that only someone who knew him as well as Julian did would be likely to notice.

Dewey snorted again and shook his head quickly before spitting onto the ground in front of the door. "Ain't been a Ranger here in thirty years," he said, "and we don't need none, either. They all left, reassigned some place down south, but no replacements ever came in. Town still maintains their station though." He paused, then turned away from the building and gestured for Raedrick and Julian to follow him into the woods. "Good riddance. Come on."

The tension went out of Julian's body in a rush, and he found himself drawing in a deep breath. Had he been holding his breath there for a minute? He was not sure.

Beside him, Raedrick's grin returned, this time far more warm and comfortable than Julian would been able to manage right then. Their eyes met.

"Surely we would have heard of their presence before now," Raedrick said in the oh-so-calm voice he used back when he was the Squad Leader.

That voice really irked Julian sometimes. He snorted. "You got worried too," he said, then turned to follow Dewey into the woods.

The bright afternoon sunlight became muted by the Glamorwood's canopy, leaving only the occasional beam of brightness streaming down to the earth below. Between the slender trunks of the evergreens, the ground lay covered in a loose layer of fallen pine needles, lending a faintly sweet aroma to the woods and muffling the trio's footsteps as they proceeded inward, and upward.

The hills that would soon become the mountains that marked Glimmer Vale's northern boundary began as just simple rolls in the terrain, but soon enough they became more steep. Before long, Julian found himself covered in sweat and breathing heavily at the effort of following Dewey higher.

And the old bastard did not seem to notice, or struggle with, the climb at all.

"Not much farther now," Dewey said over his shoulder, his tone level and his breathing slow and measured, as though he were taking a leisurely stroll along the lake.

Julian had to force himself not to grind his teeth. That would take more energy than he could afford to use, right then.

Beside him, Raedrick grunted. He looked just as wiped as Julian felt; a small comfort, that. But at Dewey's words, the weariness seemed to drain from his features, replaced by the sharp focus he always got when he was preparing for action. Julian took a deep breath and tried to follow his lead. It would not do for the

Constable to be anything but professional while on the job, after all.

They topped a particularly steep rise and stepped into a small clearing where a jagged boulder lay half-buried In the turf, surrounded by a small cluster of bushes. As he rounded the boulder, a new odor assaulted Julian's nostrils. Metallic, sickly-sweet, rancid. A mixture of the smells from a latrine and a battlefield, and beneath something else. Something...unwholesome, sickly.

He stopped, coughing as the odor seemed to hit him like a physical blow.

"Gah," Raedrick said, giving voice to Julian's thoughts.

Dewey nodded gravely. "Don't often encounter a smell like that, less'n something big's died and rotted. I figgered it was a predator's kill, but..." He gestured for them to continue onward, and pushed his way past the bushes on the other side of the boulder. Julian followed, and quickly wished he had not.

Julian was no stranger to death. He had seen it, and dealt it out, on a dozen or more battlefields. Had knelt with the dying as they gasped out their final breaths, patched up the wounded in the mud. Horror had almost become commonplace during his time in the Army, so he thought he was prepared to handle whatever Dewey had to show them. But this...

Blood was everywhere, coating the ground, the bushes, the trunks of the closest trees even though they were nearly twenty feet away. The body, if it could be called that, lay in bits and pieces, strew around as though it had been somehow ground up and then spread like manure on a farmer's field. At first glance, only the presence of torn clothing, one impossibly intact boot, and broken but recognizable hunting equipment would have even told Julian this had once been a man.

"Gods be merciful," he breathed.

Dewey shook his head. "They sure weren't to this fellow."

"Was it a bear?" Raedrick's voice was hushed, almost reverent.

The old man shook his head again. "A bear don't attack a man, not less'n he's mad or injured. An' if he did, he wouldn't leave it like this."

"Mountain lion?"

Dewey just snorted and shot Raedrick a look like he was daft. "Lions don't leave meat untouched." He gestured over to the side, past the blood splatter, where a deer carcass lay, intact and untouched except for where the hunter had evidently dressed it out before he had been killed.

Julian frowned. That made no sense. Scavengers should have made off with that carcass, or at least bitten off parts of it, by now. And Dewey was right: why would whatever killed the hunter have left the deer untouched? "What, then?" he asked.

Dewey shrugged. "Told you, ain't never seen nothing like this." He looked down at the bloodied remains and pursed his lips. "Poor bastard."

"Where's his head?" Raedrick asked.

Julian stiffened and looked around the clearing quickly. Raedrick was right. Pieces of the body were everywhere, but none of the pieces could have been the man's head. Where was it?"

Dewey scowled and pointed over Raedrick's head.

Julian turned and looked where Dewey pointed. In a little nook near the top of the boulder, higher than he could have reached if he were standing on his tip toes, lay the man's head. He was not young, but not old either; probably approaching forty. His hair was long and wavy, dark brown and pulled back from his face by a leather headband. His mouth was locked into a sound-less scream, his face frozen in a rictus of pain and utmost horror, his dark eyes wide and locked forward.

The dead man's expression made Julian's blood turn to ice water, and all the more because he recognized him from an occa-sional night at The Oarlock.

"Baelin," Julian breathed.

Dewey grunted agreement.

5

UNEXPECTED VISITOR

"**A**ny idea what did it?"

Julian swallowed a gulp of Molli's ale and lowered his mug back to the bar before he shrugged. "Animal of some kind," he replied.

His companion was an older man with dark grey hair and a matching beard who wore a cloak that was almost the same color as his hair overtop the loose-fitting garments that the fishermen of Lydelton tended to favor. He sniffed and considered that for a half minute before taking a swig himself. "Bad way to go," Horace said.

Julian nodded agreement.

The Oarlock was full to overflowing, unusual considering it was the middle of the work week. But having to go about their tasks tomorrow had not stopped people from coming out to Baelin's funeral, and afterwords to the various taverns to lift a mug in the dead man's honor.

How many even knew who he was, Julian wondered. Not many; he had kept to himself while in town, and was more often to be found out in the woods than anywhere else. The only reason Julian knew him was because they happened to both like The Oarlock.

More people knew Ilsa, of course. And a good thing, too. With Baelin gone, she would need help with their three children. Julian did not envy her the workload she had to bear.

Horace drained the last of his drink and stood up from his stool. "I'd best be off," he said. "Got a meeting with management in the morning." His lips twisted in distaste for a moment, then he grinned wryly. "Got to look respectable for them, or somesuch."

Julian snorted. "You don't have that kind of time."

Horace put on a look of feigned injury, then grinned even wider and clasped hands with Julian before turning to leave. Julian watched the old fisherman weave his way through the taproom and shook his head, amused.

His amusement faded as Horace passed a table near the door, and its occupant. The man was small, slight, easy to dismiss. He wore a black shirt, or maybe extremely dark blue, that was open at the collar and had loop earrings in both ears. His skin was past swarthy toward dark, like the men from the southern shores of the great sea, and he wore his black hair cut short around his ears and neck but longer on his crown, so that it hung to his ears almost like vines dangling over the side of a cliff.

The man's appearance was unusual enough; few people in Lydelton even approached his skin tone. But what truly drew Raedrick's eye was the staff that lay propped against the empty chair to the man's right. Long, probably longer than the man was tall, it was sanded smooth and varnished until it glinted in the light from the fireplace a few tables away.

Julian frowned. He had seen men with staves like that before, in the Army. Unless he missed his guess, the fellow was a mage, and a high-ranking one at that.

"Son of a bitch," Julian muttered.

He turned back to the bar and waved Molli over. She took a minute to fill a couple of tall tankards and set them down on one of her servers' trays before coming over with a friendly grin. "Need a refill?"

Julian was about to shake his head, but he glanced down and

saw that his mug was just about empty. "Sure, why not." He swallowed the last gulp and pushed the mug over to her.

Molli grabbed it up and retreated to the taps. A moment later she returned, foam very nearly overflowing from the top of Julian's mug. "Here you go."

Julian grinned his thanks and set a silver coin down on the bar.

Molli's eyebrow twitched upward. "Starting a tab?"

Julian nodded over toward the apparent mage's table. "When did that fellow check in?"

Molli's eyes tracked over to the newcomer's table and her grin faded slightly. "This morning, a little before noon. Why?"

Julian did not answer immediately. He took a drink while considering. The man was probably just passing through; it was not unheard-of for individuals to travel the mountain passes alone in the summertime, though it was not common. If he did not linger, it would probably not be a problem, but all the same... "Did he say how long he's staying?"

Molli's grin faded completely, becoming a concerned frown as she regarded Julian. "No, but he paid enough for a week." She added a bit more force to her words. "Why?"

Julian sighed and stood up, taking his mug with him. "He's a mage," he said. Molli's eyebrow quirked upward, but he could see she did not understand the issue. "Send over another of whatever he's drinking, will you?"

She nodded, and Julian turned away. As he walked over to the stranger, he felt almost as though he was getting ready for battle.

He weaved past several intervening tables, watching the mage carefully as he went. The man appeared to be taking his ease, munching on a plate of Molli's signature fishcakes and watching the goings on around him with an expression of mild amusement. And why not? People watching could be entertaining, especially when they had some drink on. But as he got closer, Julian noted that the amusement on the mage's face did not translate over to his eyes, which were sharp, watchful. Piercing.

The mage noted Julian's approach and turned to regard him, his eyes tracing up and down Julian's body in a quick once-over that lingered on the badge of office he wore. Something in the mage's demeanor shifted upon seeing the badge, becoming more stiff in a subtle way that Julian probably would not have noticed had he not been watching.

"Constable," the mage said by way of greeting, and inclined his head politely.

Well, the badge was good for something at least. "Good evening," Julian said, and gestured toward the other empty seat at the mage's table. Not the one holding his staff upright. "Mind if I join you for a moment?" He smiled, to show he meant no imposition.

"Of course," replied the mage. "Always happy to make the acquaintance of a public servant."

Julian smirked as he sat. "Don't know I'd call myself that." He set his mug down and held out his hand to the mage. "Julian Hinderbrook."

The mage looked at his hand for a second before clasping it. "Loran Haversted."

"We don't get many members of the Magestirium coming through," Julian said, still grinning. "Just figured I'd welcome you to town."

Loran's eyebrows lifted, in surprise, Julian was sure. "Not many people in places like this would know a member of the Magestirium by sight." The question, unstated, hung in the air for a moment.

Julian shrugged and took a sip from his mug. "Haven't always lived here."

"Ah."

A serving girl came around to the table, carrying a glass that was halfway filled with an amber fluid on her tray. She made a shallow curtsy and set the glass down in front of Loran, then turned away to continue her rounds.

"Miss, I - "

"It's on me," Julian interjected.

Loran looked at Julian through narrowed eyes for a moment, then inclined his head in a seated half-bow. "Thank you," he said blandly.

"My pleasure. So," Julian took another sip before continuing, "I'm sure the Mayor would love to meet you, give his regards to your order, that sort of thing. Will you be in town long?"

A slight shrug of his shoulders preceded Loran's reply. "Just long enough to see my business through, then I will be off."

"And what business is that?"

Loran's eyes hardened. "None of yours, Constable, I assure you."

That was plain enough. Fine, if that was how he wanted to play it... "I don't mean to pry," Julian said, redoubling his efforts at grinning. "The Mayor's a busy man, as you know. I wouldn't want him to miss the opportunity to say hello."

The drink Julian bought lay on the table between them, untouched. Loran never looked at it, just at Julian, his gaze intent, probing. Julian made a point of not meeting his eyes directly. Rumor had it that a mage could read your thoughts if he looked into your eyes for too long, and that would not do at all, if the rumor was true. He would have to ask Melanie about that when he saw her...

Damnit. Don't go there.

Finally Loran smiled again, ever so slightly. "I expect I will be in town for two or three days, maybe a short while longer. I trust that will give the Mayor sufficient time to clear his schedule?"

Julian nodded. "Almost certainly. I'll have the Mayor's office leave word with Mistress Millens as to the best time. If that will suffice?"

Loran nodded, more a gesture of concession to an inferior than an agreement between equals. Julian had to stop himself from scowling in annoyance at the sheer arrogance of it.

"Well then, I'll leave you to your entertainment." Julian stood and made a half-bow to the mage, his grin still plastered to his face.

"Thank you, Constable. I look forward to our next meeting."

Not really, Loran's eyes said.

Julian turned away and walked back to the bar. There, he drained the rest of his mug in a long, smooth swallow, then he set it down and turned to leave the Inn. It was not until the front door swung shut behind him that he realized he had just left Molli and her girls one hell of a tip.

Oh well. He had more pressing matters to attend to. He just hoped Melanie would be sensible about this.

6

THE DOWN LOW

R aedrick knocked once, then pushed open the door to Melanie's Mystical Crafts and stepped inside. Julian followed on his heels, a sense of urgency competing with profound reluctance for dominance in his head. How Melanie would react to Loran's presence was hard to say, but in her place Julian would probably be packing to leave town fairly quickly. The Magestirium did not deal kindly with outsiders who practiced their craft, and Melanie, as a woman, was an outsider by definition.

Julian was not sure what irked him more: the stupidity of that policy or the thought of Melanie leaving.

They had become good friends over the last several months. Well, friends anyway. Or maybe trusted acquaintances and colleagues. Or something. Regardless, it would be hard to see Melanie go, even if it was necessary for her own protection.

And she had done so well for herself here.

Her shop lay at the northeastern edge of town, away from the Lake and from casual attention from non-locals. The small building had once been an old spinster's house, but it had fallen vacant when the poor woman passed on, in late Spring. There had been a small squabble among her surviving relatives—two brothers with enough wrinkles between them to make a prune appear smooth—over who would get the house afterwords. Melanie had solved that by plopping down enough coin to satisfy them both, and that was that. She had to have paid more than the place was worth, though she denied it. Although Julian supposed maybe the two brothers were secretly relieved to put the silly conflict behind them. Regardless, it was a quick transaction, and within a few weeks Melanie opened up her shop.

The door swung shut behind Julian and he paused for a moment, taking in the ambience. Symbols and words of power, or at least of spiritual significance, decorated the walls, up high near where they joined with the ceiling. Bottles containing remedies and the like rested upon a shelf off to the right. Directly across from the door, pendants and other trinkets, all bearing penta-grams or other symbols of power, were on display. A small book-shelf sat in the middle of the shop, partially full with tomes that were decorated with strange texts and symbols. The heavy odor of incense lay over it all, from the burner which sat behind the counter to the left, on top of a strongbox that Melanie claimed held her most rare, powerful, and valuable, items.

Julian had to hand it to Melanie; she did not play around. She aimed for mystical, and went well past it to almost weird. Not that he would ever tell her that straight out. The memory of a quartet of mounted men and their horses suddenly erupting into flame with the flick of her wrist sprang to mind. Best not to make her really angry.

Julian snorted to himself; that was just silly. They were friends, after all.

Nevertheless, he could not help but remember the strength and power that lay beneath Melanie's decidedly appealing exte-rior. Her feminine wiles concealed a deadly and cunning oppo-nent, if one was unfortunate enough to get on her bad side.

"Where is -"

No sooner had the words left Raedrick's lips than Melanie

stepped into the shop from a small doorway in the left rear corner, behind the counter, that was enclosed by hanging beads.

Tall and lush, Melanie was, as always, dressed impeccably. Today she wore a flowing dark-blue gown that was cut tight at her waist and flared below her hips. The collar was ruffled in a lighter shape of blue, almost white, and cut low enough to reveal a hint of her impressive cleavage. A simple black leather belt with a silver clasp, from which hung a small knife that rested over her left hip, set off the dress and further accentuated her curves. A silver necklace and earrings completed her ensemble. Wavy dark-brown hair hung just past her shoulders, and her eyes, just slightly lighter in color than her dress, shone with intellect and confidence.

"Well, well," Melanie said in her melodious alto, "my two favorite law men." She smiled warmly, an eyebrow quirking upward to accentuate the teasing tone she took. "To what do I owe this pleasure?"

Raedrick shared a glance with Julian, then cleared his throat. "Not sure it's a pleasure this time."

Melanie's smile faded slightly, but she remained silent, her eyes questioning.

"A mage from the Magestirium is in town. Checked into The Oarlock yesterday, and he looks to stay for a while."

The smile left Melanie's face completely and she looked from Raedrick to Julian, the questioning look more intense, if anything. He nodded in confirmation. And now for the panic.

He should have known better.

Melanie looked gravely at the two of them for a moment, then said, "Who?"

Raedrick blinked and looked at Julian meaningfully for a moment, then nodded. As though he was not going to tell her.

"Loran Haversted," Julian said levelly.

Melanie nodded and looked away. She licked her lips as she thought for a moment.

Then she burst out laughing.

Julian traded another look with Raedrick. The former squad leader scrunched up his eyes the way he always did when he got confused. Julian could not say he blamed him. The Magestirium was famously protective of its secrets. No one, especially a woman, would be allowed to walk free once learning them. Loran was a clear and present danger to Melanie's wellbeing. And yet, she laughed.

And kept on laughing for a full minute. Finally, she stopped and wiped the beginnings of tears from her eyes. Tears of mirth, of course. Then, shaking her head, she said, "Honestly, boys, do you think I've never been in the same town as a member of the Magestirium before?"

"Well," Raedrick began.

"We just thought," Julian said at the same time.

Melanie rolled her eyes in annoyance. "Don't worry about him. I'll be fine."

She was capable, that was for sure. But this was a serious problem. She must not have understood. "You don't understand. This guy - "

Melanie's eyes flashed to anger in an instant, and she fixed Julian with a glare that stopped his words in his throat. "No, *you* don't understand. Those...men..." she said the word like a pejorative "see only what they wish to see. Women cannot be mages, so they are not. All a woman must do is surround herself with the superstitious trappings of a cottage wise woman, or whatever they call them in whatever shanty town they happen to be in, and the Magestirium will just see a peddler of nonsense and think nothing more of it."

Julian chewed on that for a moment, and looked back around the shop again. Come to think of it, most of the products Melanie had up on display strongly resembled others he had seen in any number of home remedy shops, fortune tellers' parlors, and the like. He found himself pursing his lips in appreciation as he really saw the place for what it was: a quite convincing front.

Except...

"People in town know you're more than just some woman selling herbs in water that don't do anything," Raedrick said. "They've seen you work."

Melanie sniffed and waved a dismissive hand. "This isn't a grand metropolis, Raedrick." Her eyes flicked toward Julian and some of her smile reappeared. "You acknowledged that when you asked me to stay. No better place to hide than in a small town, isn't that what you said?"

Julian swallowed, the concern still heavy in his chest. "Yes, but I didn't mean - "

"Ask yourself this. How likely do you think the people in this town are to sell out someone who they know is responsible for saving their homes and families from depredation, and who they know can exact terrible vengeance upon them if they do?"

Another good point. If anything, the people of Lydelton looked at Melanie with even more awe than they did Raedrick and Julian, and that was saying something. And they were good, honest, hardworking folk, for the most part. Julian found himself nodding in understanding, and agreement.

"They would not. Not if they could help it."

Melanie returned the nod, her smile growing ever so slightly. "I have been discrete in the aid I've lent since the battle. No one has borne witness save the people I've helped, and the things I've done were personal enough that they won't come forward to tell about them, I assure you."

Raedrick looked abashed, probably no less than Julian did. He felt like enough of an ass, anyway. Of course Melanie would know how to hide in plain sight. She had been doing it for... Come to think of it, Julian had no idea how long she had been on the run before she settled here in Lydelton. It was probably just as well.

"Alright," Raedrick said, trying to regain some authority, or at least dignity, with his tone. "Just wanted you to know he was here, so you can take steps." He gave her a rather lame-looking smile.

Melanie rolled her eyes again, but her smile became more warm. "I appreciate your concern." She glanced at Julian and her smile widened a hair. "Both of you. But I'm a big girl. I can take care of myself."

There was not much else to say in response, so Julian did not bother to try. Neither did Raedrick. A few moments later, they hit the streets again. By his expression, Raedrick felt just as silly as Julian did. Some heroes they were.

Melanie pushed the door shut behind Raedrick and Julian. The click of the latch seemed to echo through the small front room of her shop, conveying a sense of finality.

Of doom.

She sagged against the door and her head fell limply against its surface. Fear, anger, despair, and a red-hot desire for vengeance all battled within her for a long moment. Unbidden, tears left her eyes and ran down her cheeks, then dropped and fell to the floor with inaudible splats that seemed to echo through her consciousness.

Loran was here.

Melanie drew a deep breath, trying to get control of herself. She was better than this. Timon had taught her better. But try though she might, the only things she could think of were the last time she saw Timon, bound and gagged, his eyes tight with agony as the Magestirium's questioners began their work on him, and the look on the Vigilant's face: beatific, full of a righteous ecstasy that only the most fanatical, most hateful of people could attain.

She wanted to kill him.

She needed to flee from him.

Melanie let her breath out, and, unbidden, a loud sob escaped her lips. Before she knew it, she was weeping. Weeping for her lost love, who had risked and, in the end, given everything so that her curiosity could be sated. And weeping for herself. She had dared to hope that here she could find refuge. Here she could find peace, and maybe happiness. And perhaps even love.

But no longer.

The man who killed Timon was here, and he would find her. And then he would kill her, brutally and without mercy. Of that, Melanie had no doubt.

The notion of flight crossed her mind, and she shrugged it away. Fleeing never helped those the Magestirium set out to destroy, not once the Inquisitors had their scent. It was only a matter of when and where. The only reason she had lived long enough to get here was because Timon had kept quiet about her. He must have; of that she had no doubt.

But they would be looking for a woman who practiced Magery, and word must have gotten out from somewhere that there was such a woman here in Lydelton. She was caught. Well and truly caught; the noose just had not tightened yet.

Unless she could turn the tables.

Melanie blinked away the tears and lifted her head off of the wooden planks that made up her shop's door. She had not considered that. Perhaps Vigilant Haversted had not yet fully discerned her location. If that were the case, he may not yet be ready to strike.

He would be unprepared. Vulnerable.

Melanie's lips turned slightly upwards as the thought lifted some of her despair. She may yet be able to salvage the situation. But she would have to move quickly.

❧ 7 ❧

DEATH'S DOOR

" **C**onstable!"

A woman's high-pitched scream stopped Julian in his tracks. He was walking down Water Street, one of the three imaginatively named main roads that led down to the docks from Main Street, heading toward the Covington Brothers' warehouse in his normal mid-morning round of the various businesses in town. Julian had just been thinking it was well past time Raedrick took a turn at this particular check—the warehouse was...fragrant...from the multitudes of fish that had been processed there over the years—but for one reason or another he always begged off on it. And so it was not without a certain sense of relief that Julian turned around to face the woman calling for him.

The relief faded as soon as he saw the woman sprinting down the road toward him. She wore a plain yellow dress, with a white sash around her waist that was embroidered with yellow, blue, and pink flowers, and simple white shoes, almost slippers. Her graying hair was done up in a bun atop her head, and she wore no makeup. Julian recognized her at once: Helena, Beverlee the teacher's sister.

She was old for his taste, but Julian had to admit she had kept

herself up well through the years. Like her sister, she was a spinster and there were all sorts of rumors around town about her.
About both of them. The sorts of rumors that were primarily
spoken by women in half-whispers where they imagined men
could not hear them. Of course, the rumors got around anyway.
Julian did his best to pay them no heed, but he still caught himself
wondering sometimes.

This was not one of those times. The look on Helena's face—
horrified beyond reason, desperately hopeful and yet also full of
despair—would have sent any such frivolous thoughts from his
mind even if her tone had not.

Helena slid to a stop in front of him, gasping for air for a
moment. Julian put a hand on her shoulder to steady her. "What's
wrong?"

"Beverlee," Helena gasped. "She's..." She gasped again, then
clapped her hand to her mouth as though suddenly realizing
what she was about to say. The desperation and fear on her face
gave way to grief and loss so profound that it looked as though it
shattered everything else in her, and she let out a little wail.

Her knees buckled, and Julian had to move quickly to catch
her before she hit the ground. The little wail become a long and
guttural scream of denial, loss, bitterness. Pain. She clung to him
like a drowning man clinging to a scrap of wood and shivered,
her chest heaving as her scream gave way to sobs, then full on
weeping that seemed as though it would never end.

Julian's heart sank to the ground at his feet. He did not need to
ask what had happened; it was obvious. Helena's sister was dead.
He held her close, letting her cry.

Two deaths in less than a week. This was not good.

Beverlee and Helena lived in a small flat atop a house near the
eastern edge of town. Not too far from the final battle between
Lydelton and Isenholf's band of brigands, earlier this year. The

building was far enough into town that Julian and Raedrick had not imposed on the landlord to erect scaffolding for archers, or to erect a barricade alongside his house. But the landlord none-theless tried, once or twice, to boast of his proximity to the fight over a pint or two of ale.

But only once or twice. The glares of the men who had actually been there, and the names of the men who had fallen, spoken by his neighbors, silenced his words better than any threat could have.

The house was stoutly built and not overly pretty. But then, it did not have to be. The stairs up to the flat were sturdy, though uncovered, so the sisters had to endure the elements on their way up and down from their home, even in the depths of winter, which in Glimmer Vale could be bitter indeed.

As Julian tramped up the stairs, he glanced behind at Helena, who waited on the street below with haunted, sunken eyes that were red from tears. His heart went out to her, and not just for her loss. A woman alone in the world faced a challenging life. It would have been difficult enough with her sister by her side. But now...

He shook his head. "It's just not right," he murmured.

Raedrick, leading the way up the stairs, nodded concurrence. "Is it ever?"

Julian had no answer to that.

The stairs doubled back upon themselves and ended at a simple wooden doorway that jutted out form the peaked roof of the building as though daring the winter's snow to cause it trouble. A foul odor permeated the landing, the smell of rotting meat and corruption.

It took a moment for Raedrick to get the key to work in the lock; the landlord had apparently not seen to any maintenance on the lock in some time. Although, if there were any things that required attention, the lock becoming more difficult to open would likely rate near the last on the list. Finally, Raedrick got the door open, and the stench hit them even like a jab from a pugilist.

It was bad enough with the door closed. Now that it was open... Julian almost gagged at the smell.

This was going to be bad.

Raedrick looked no more eager that Julian felt. They shared a resigned look, then stepped inside.

The flat was more spacious than Julian expected from looking at the building from the outside. A good-sized living area, with a serviceable kitchen nook off to the left, greeted them as they entered. A pair of closed doors, nearly identical in their dark-stained wood, stood opposite the entrance, no doubt leading to the sisters' bedrooms. The living area was simply furnished with a stout wooden table in the middle and a pair of chairs toward the front of the house, where a broad window, framed by drapes that were embroidered with cheery forest scenes involving horses and other small animals strutting through the trees, let in a greater than average amount of light from the outside. A small bookshelf stood along the far wall, about two-thirds of the way filled with tomes of various sorts, and the kitchen was well stocked with utensils and foodstuffs. It was warmly decorated with rugs on the floors and paintings, many obviously from children's' hands, all over the walls. The sisters loved children, and it showed. Strange that neither chose to have any of her own.

It was a good home. Neat, warm, with all the charm and appeal of a well-lived-in place that oozed good feelings and simple contentment.

As long as you did not look at what was on the table.

Beverlee had not been dead for very long, but already the day's heat had crept up into the flat and things had begun to go rancid. Not to mention the things that happen to a body soon after its death. Julian had seen it on a dozen or more battlefields, the body's muscles letting go once its spirit had left, letting its filth fall where it may.

There was never dignity in death, but some people should not be degraded like that. Beverlee was one of those; she had given her whole life to the children of Lydelton.

If the normal after-death loosening of the bowels was all that had befallen her, it would have been bad enough. But this...

"Gods above," Raedrick breathed, his face ashen and his tone matching it, if a man's tone could be said to have a color. "It's just like with Baelin."

Julian nodded his head mutely, struggling to take it all in.

The table was strewn with body parts. Little bits and pieces here and there, some recognizable as a hand or part of a leg, but many of them too savaged to tell. But just like with the woodsman, the head was clearly gone, missing from the rest entirely.

It rested upon the curved outlet of the small wood-fired stove that dominated the kitchen area, nestled onto a bend in the pipe not far from where it ran out through the building's roof. Beverlee wore almost exactly the same expression Baelin had: eyes locked wide open in a horrified stare, her mouth wide as though trying to scream, and her expression past terror to a fear so primal that it defied immediate description.

"Bugger me," Julian managed, finally.

Raedrick did not respond. His initial shock had faded, and he was beginning to look around with more of his normal manner, his face set in a stern mask.

This was bad. Julian had thought that already, but it was more true than he figured he knew. And one thing was certain.

"This was not the work of an animal."

Raedrick had taken the words right out of his mouth. Julian nodded agreement. "Animal that could do this would not have made it into town without anyone noticing." He took a deep breath, through his mouth so as to avoid as much of the stench as he could. "Which means..."

Raedrick finished the though. "Whoever did this also killed Baelin." He turned and looked gravely at Julian, his blue eyes seeming two or three shades darker than normal in the grisly room. "We're looking for a man."

Julian nodded agreement. Though he could not imagine the kind of man who would do something like this.

FORMALITIES

Mayor Brimly's scowl seemed to take up his entire face. He sat behind his massive wooden desk in his office on the upper floor of City Hall—though city was perhaps a bit of a stretch—and looked at Julian and Raedrick through narrowed eyes that gleamed with concern. So did the sweat that ran down his brow and along the line of his chin to pool at its tip before dropping with a silent splat onto the blotter that lay atop his desk.

The mayor was somewhat more than plump. As usual, he wore his badge of office, a golden fish jumping out of the water, prominently on the left breast of his summer jacket. Today, the jacket was off-white, just the slightest shade of yellow, with a collared white shirt beneath. Julian had not seen his leggings yet, but no doubt his attire was perfectly matched. His wife always saw to that.

Julian had no desire for a wife like that. He would not dream of dictating a lady's choice of attire, as long as it lay within the bounds of decency. Why should a lady make such demands of him, or any man?

Stupid question, right there.

"Are you sure it's the same thing as Baelin?"

Raedrick kept his face smooth, neutral and respectful, but Julian knew it was only with difficulty. The Mayor could be...trying...at the best of times. But when things got stressful, he was not the most steady of individuals.

"Completely," Raedrick replied. "The bodies were arranged almost identically."

Mayor Brimly blew out a long exhalation and turned in his chair—it was set on a pivot, a nicely made contraption—to look out the window behind his desk, scowling. "People are not going to take this well."

Of course not. Though not universally well-respected—women who seemed to spurn even the idea of marriage stood out and were not well regarded by some—Beverlee was at least appreciated for the services she provided to the town's children. Or at least that portion of the town's children that she had the time to take under her wing. And whose parents were able to meet her price.

Come to think of it, there were likely some people in town, more than a few, who may have held a grudge against poor Beverlee and her sister, for just that reason.

But that was not what the mayor was getting at.

He looked back at the two of them. "I want this kept quiet."

Julian blinked and traded a glance with Raedrick.

"That will be...difficult," Raedrick said. "Plenty of people know Beverlee is dead already."

Mayor Brimly snorted softly and waved a dismissive hand. "I don't mean the fact that she's dead." He leaned forward, his face grim. "I mean how she died. And how it compares with Baelin. If people start putting two and two together, we'll have neighbor suspicious of neighbor. Before you know it, folks will start accusing each other for all to hear. Then there'll be fighting." He shook his head. "We need to avoid that."

"I doubt it'll come to that," Julian said.

Mayor Brimly snorted more loudly and scowled at him.

"You've not been here that long. Trust me, this place will go up like a haystack if we let it."

Julian frowned. He was not so sure about Mayor Brimly's appraisal there. The people of Lydelton could have broken, fractured, when Isenholf's brigands put the pressure on. But instead, men went against their employers' wishes to fight alongside he and Raedrick, the populace at large hunkered down and helped out as best they could, and the town in general pulled together.

But that was against an external existential threat. How well would they stick together if it had been one of their own working against the rest of them?

Suddenly the Mayor's concern did not seem quite so far fetched. Damnit.

Raedrick frowned as well, and Julian could tell he was thinking along the same lines. Slowly, he nodded to the Mayor, conceding the point. "I'll talk with the people who have seen the body so far. It was only Helena, their landlord, and the priest's assistants. I think I can convince them to keep quiet."

Mayor Brimly nodded, his expression still grave. "I hope so."

A knock on the door to the Mayor's office interrupted the rest of his words. Mayor Brimly cocked his head at the door for a second, as though considering whether to answer. Then his eyes flickered over to the clock that rested on a shelf between two windows on the wall facing Main Street and he blanched.

"Come."

The door swung halfway open and the Mayor's secretary, a slight woman in her early middle years who wore her red-blond hair short, barely clearing her ears in back, stuck her head in. "Magester Haversted here to see you, Master Mayor."

Mayor Brimly grunted and shoved himself to his feet. "Send him in, Frieda," he said as he rose.

Julian and Raedrick stood with him. Julian could not help but watch as the door swung open fully and Loran strode confidently into the room. He was dressed more formally this day, in flowing robes that reached his feet and were a blue so dark they could almost be mistaken for black. A golden medallion hung around his neck, supporting the symbol of the Magestirium on his chest. It seemed to glow with an internal light. Neat trick.

Loran ignored the two law men as he entered, his gaze instead fixed completely on the Mayor. He strode to the front of Mayor Brimly's desk with a smooth, confident gait that seemed more fitting for a ballroom than a small office, and never mind the staff in his right hand, then inclined his head in greeting. "Master Mayor, it is a pleasure," he said in a formal, courtly tone.

Mayor Brimly perked up at Loran's demeanor. By the time the mage had finished greeting him, the Mayor's chest puffed out and he almost seemed to preen. He always was one to be impressed with a good show.

"The pleasure is mine, Magester Haversted," Mayor Brimly replied as he made a half-bow from his waist in response to Loran's greeting. "Lydelton is honored to welcome an esteemed member of the Magestirium to our midst."

Loran merely smiled, the kind of smile that said he was accepting a just supplication from one inferior to himself. It set Julian's teeth on edge.

"I believe you have met our Constables already," Mayor Brimly said, gesturing to Julian, then to Raedrick.

Loran cast only the briefest of glances at Julian, and he thought he saw the mage's lips twist in the tiniest of smirks there for a second, before turning his attention upon Raedrick. He, Loran studied intently for a brief moment, and Julian got the impression he had taken Raedrick's measure completely before Loran smiled and made the slightest of nods toward him.

"I have already met Constable Hinderbrook," he said, "but I am pleased to make your acquaintance." One eyebrow quirked upward, questioningly.

"Raedrick Baletier."

Raedrick held his hand out, and for a second Julian thought Loran was not going to take it. Then he clasped hands with Raedrick in the way a soldier greets a man he has fought beside.

Raedrick's eyebrows quirked upward in surprise, but he returned the shake in a like manner.

"A pleasure, Constable Baletier," Loran said. His eyes flickered downward quickly. "It is most unusual for a man of your heritage to carry a Tyrashi blade."

Julian blinked in surprise and his gaze shifted unconsciously to the sword that hung from Raedrick's left hip. Slightly curved, with a hand-and-a-half hilt, it was a far cry from the saber he used to wield. Longer, heavier, and far more elegant, at least to Julian's eyes. It had belonged to Selam, a citizen of Lydelton who like them had come here from elsewhere. Selam died protecting the town from Isenholf's brigands, and had bequeathed the blade to Raedrick. It was some sort of family heirloom, but Raedrick had never explained its significance fully and Julian had not pushed. Raedrick and Selam had fought together, forged a sort-of friendship together, and that was not something that Julian felt comfortable shoving his nose into.

That said, he had never heard Selam say where he came from. If he was Tyrashi...

Come to think of it, Julian still had no idea where Tyrash was. He never had gone back to Melanie to find out.

Raedrick cleared his throat, his left hand coming to rest on the hilt of his sword almost unconsciously. "A gift from a friend," he said, simply.

Loran's eyebrows lifted high onto his forehead for a second. "A very generous gift." His eyes never left the sword. His tongue flicked across his teeth as though tasting something sweet, and Julian got a distinct sense of avarice from the man. "Unless I miss my guess, that is Farelio's workmanship."

Raedrick blinked, confused, but Julian beat him to the question.

"Who?"

The mage looked back at him and truly did smirk this time. "Tell me you've not heard of Farelio? He was one of the greatest swordsmiths of the last half-millenium." He shook his head slightly, then turned back to Raedrick. "May I see the blade?"

Raedrick hesitated, his expression doubtful.

"Come now. I only wish to see if his mark is upon it." His tone and expression shouted that Raedrick would be beyond silly to refuse the request.

Raedrick glanced from Loran to Julian, who shrugged; what could it hurt? Then, with the soft sound of metal dragging against hardened leather, Raedrick pulled the sword out and held it upright between himself and Loran, turned so the mage could see the flat of the blade.

Julian had seen the sword many times, but its elegance and beauty never ceased to amaze him. The blade was curved and honed to a razor-edge on the entire convex side, as well as on the last third of the concave so its wielder could cut with a backswing almost as easily as with a front. That was not so terribly unusual; Julian had seen one or two blades of similar design. What set Selam's—Raedrick's—sword apart were the intricate engravings on the flat of the blade. Running the entire length of the blade, except along the cutting surfaces, they interlocked in a construct of artistry that rivaled anything Julian had ever seen.

The sword's effect on Loran was impressive, well beyond what Julian would have expected. The mage's eyes widened and his breath caught in his throat. He stood speechless for a full minute as his eyes traced the engravings on the blade, his expression clearly that of a man who cannot believe what he is seeing. He reached out as if to touch it.

Raedrick, frowning slightly, pulled the sword away and said, "Careful, Magester. It's very sharp." Then he re-sheathed it with a single smoothly-practiced movement.

Loran blinked, then flashed a rueful smile and chuckled softly. "Of course." He drew a deep breath and inclined his head toward Raedrick, a bit more deeply this time. "That is a princely gift, Constable Baletier. I would be sure to keep a close eye on it, were I you." He quirked an eyebrow upward slightly, then turned to face

Mayor Brimly fully, who stood looking more than a little confused.

"Now then, Master Mayor, I believe we have business to discuss."

Mayor Brimly nodded, wiping the confusion from his face with practiced ease and replacing it with an ingratiating smile. "Yes, of course." He glanced at Raedrick, then Julian. "Thank you, gentlemen."

The dismissal was plain. Raedrick inclined his head to the Mayor. "Master Mayor," he said, then nodded to Loran again. "Magester."

The Mage returned the nod peremptorily, though his eyes flicked back to Raedrick's sword again, ever so briefly.

Julian said his farewells quickly then followed his friend from the office and pulled the Mayor's heavy wooden door shut behind them. "Well," he said, "that was interesting."

Raedrick smirked slightly and made a little shrug, but Julian could see the wheels turning behind his eyes. Loran knew something about his newly acquired sword. Something Raedrick did not, and it was going to eat away at him until he figured it out.

✿ 9 ✿

SAYING GOODBYE

They wasted no time on Beverlee's funeral, same as with Baelin.

No sense in putting it off any longer than necessary, especially with the bodies in the state they were. And so that very evening, Helena led a long procession—almost as long as the procession for the men who died fighting Isenholf—down to the docks, where her sister's body lay wrapped in clean cloths that covered her from head to toe in a small boat.

The cloths were a necessity because of the state her body was in. But they were not unheard-of in any case. Some families preferred to look on their dead one last time, but many did not. And sometimes there was enough of a delay before the ceremony that decay began to set in, and it would not do for the guests to see the deceased in that state. So no comments were made at Beverlee being made up that way.

At least not openly. But Julian saw the looks between individuals in the crowd, the furtive whispers, the speculative expressions. Everyone was wondering about the similarity with Baelin's funeral, just a couple days before. It did not take a mental heavyweight to wonder whether she had been murdered in the same way he had, and if that were the case it was not an animal that did him, was it?

He could practically see the rumors that Mayor Brimly warned he and Raedrick about beginning to take form.

The ceremony was quick, as Helena apparently wanted it. Mayor Brimly said a few words, which was appropriate for a woman who had contributed to the youth of the town for so long, and then men hoisted the boat's sail and cast it off from the dock.

The breeze caught the sail, pushing the boat further from shore. When it got about a hundred feet out, a man knocked an arrow and dipped the head into a torch, setting it alight. Then he aimed and shot, and the arrow tracked across the sky to the boat, where the carefully prepared wood caught fire quickly. It burned for several minutes before the boat sank beneath the still waters of Lake Glimmermere.

Then the crowd began to break up, and before long the only people remaining on the dock were Helena, Raedrick, and Julian. She just watched the patch of water where her sister sank down to her final rest in silence. They did not intrude upon her grief.

QUESTIONS AND QUESTIONS

"There has to be some connection between Baelin and Beverlee."

Julian sipped at his drink and frowned as he turned Raedrick's words over in his head. After a moment, he shrugged. "Does there?"

Raedrick gave him a long-suffering look, the kind that made people feel stupid.

"Don't look at me like that," Julian said. "Could be there's nothing in common between them, and this is all just..."

"Random?" Raedrick finished for him. He picked up the knife lying next to his plate and cut off a piece of his fish, then began chewing rapidly. He swallowed and made a jabbing motion with the knife, toward Julian. "You don't really believe that, do you?"

Julian sighed and leaned back in his seat. He turned his head to look out over the taproom at The Oarlock, where they were taking their lunch. It was a good-sized crowd today, the day after Beverlee's funeral. Cobblers, smiths, workmen of all sorts, and a few ladies who worked the trades as well, were sitting in small groups of twos or threes at tables scattered around the room. A good crowd, but the boisterous conversation that normally filled the taproom was muted. There was a tension in the air, an unspoken worry that seemed to have lowered everyone's spirits.

Two people were dead, and despite his and Raedrick's efforts to stem rumors over the last day since their meeting with the Mayor, enough people had begun to put two and two together that Beverlee had been murdered. Folks were beginning to worry that there might be another incident. And if so, who would be next? Why?

The mood was not contained within The Oarlock's walls either. Julian had sensed it, more diluted but still there, in the people as he made his rounds this morning. People were worried, afraid. He had not seen the town worked up like this since Isenholf.

Julian looked back at his plate and jammed a cut of fish into his mouth and forced himself to chew it, not even noticing the spicy deliciousness that was Molli's signature recipe. In truth, he hoped the two murders were related somehow. It would be much more difficult to figure out who was responsible if there were no link between the two victims.

All the same, though, Baelin? And Beverlee? He could not imagine how they would have crossed paths, except in passing.

"Rae, Baelin did not have the money to have anyone but Ilsa teach his children, and Beverlee never really had anything to do with the men in town except for business. What connection could there be?"

"I don't know. But there has to be something. Maybe Ilsa and Beverlee..."

Julian shook his head. "I asked Helena. They were passing acquaintances, nothing more."

"Well that just..." Raedrick dropped his knife and threw his hands up, helplessly.

"Yeah."

They sat in silence. Julian was certain he looked as puzzled, frustrated, and worried as Raedrick did. He certainly felt it.

The serving girl, a slight little brunette named Sophie who

wore the standard blue dress and apron that Molli made all her girls wear at work, came by a minute or so later. She paused, looking suddenly uncertain, as she saw their faces. For a second, Julian thought she was going to turn and leave, but instead she visibly collected herself and coughed slightly.

"Can I get you anything else, Constables?"

Raedrick gave a little jerk as though startled. He truly had been lost in his thoughts, if he had not noticed her arrival. He flushed slightly under Julians gaze, then smiled abashedly and shook his head to the girl. "I'm fine, thank you."

The serving girl looked at Julian, and he shook his head also. She paused, biting her lip for a moment, then glanced around furtively before asking in a low voice, "Do you know who did it yet?"

Julian blinked. That was unexpected. Though perhaps it should not have been. He traded glances with Raedrick, then cleared his throat before answering, "Can't really talk about that, Sophie."

"In other words, no."

She was no dummy. But then, Julian had seen Sophie befuddle many a man in this taproom. Granted, most times those men were more than a little tipsy, but she had always been quick of wit. He sighed. "We're working on it," he began.

Sophie nodded slowly. "I hope so. Beverlee and her sister taught me when I was younger. What happened to her was so... What kind of beast would do such a thing?" Her voice broke and she looked down at the floor, her face pale, sorrowful. Fearful.

Son of a bitch. Julian looked over at Raedrick, scowling. It looked like their attempts at rumor control had failed worse than they thought.

"It'll be all right, miss," Raedrick said, in that comforting tone that he did so much better than Julian. "You'll see."

Sophie put on a brave smile, but her eyes said she doubted it. She bobbed a little curtsy and went on about her rounds. Julian followed her with his gaze, and not just because of the wonderful way her hips swayed when she walked.

"So what's the plan?"

Raedrick said, darkly, "I'm working on it."

Back in Beverlee and Helena's flat.

It still stank, though the odor had lost much of its punch. The landlord had left the windows fully open through the night; Helena had stayed with friends. Small wonder why. There was no way Julian could have been convinced to stay there another minute, were he in her shoes.

He looked around the flat's interior and found himself shying away from the table where Beverlee's corpse had lain. He told himself to grow a spine, not shy away. But he found he almost expected to see her lying there when he looked, and worse, lying there staring at him with accusation in her eyes.

I am dead and I should not be. What kind of law man are you, to let this happen?

Julian blanched and looked further away from the table toward the chairs on either side of a small window that looked down at the street in front of the house. He almost did not realize he was avoiding looking until Raedrick cleared his throat.

Julian looked at his friend and noted the quirked eyebrow, the knowing stare for a moment before he shrugged, ever so slightly. "I'll look over here."

Raedrick smirked and for a moment Julian thought he was going to sling a verbal barb his way, but then he just nodded and stepped over to the little kitchenette. He began opening cupboard doors, looking in containers, intent on his search.

Julian's search of the living area took only a few minutes. As far as he could tell there was nothing out of place, or unusual to be found. A small stack of books between the chairs, mostly for learning but a few that had obviously come from one of the more recent caravans; no one in these parts penned stories about fainting damsels and unbelievably handsome and gallant princes.

Julian snorted. A gallant prince. That would be the day.

He turned to find Raedrick with his arms crossed and a frown on his lips. His right index finger tapped absently on the meat of his left forearm. "Anything?"

Julian shook his head and turned toward Helena's bedroom door. He hated to intrude on her privacy. Again. They had not found anything during their search yesterday afternoon. But maybe they had overlooked something. There had to be *something* pointing to why she had been killed.

He was just pushing the door open when a tentative knock at the flat's front door brought him up cold.

Julian spun around and blinked when he found his sword hand on the grip of his blade. He did not really expect trouble *here*? Did he?

A tall, plump man stood in the entrance doorway, his hand still raised against the open door where he had just finished knocking. He was an elderly man, old really, with thin wisps of silver hair that struggled mightily to cover the gleaming pate that was the majority of his head. His clothing was the kind of modest quality that bespoke a moderately successful tradesman who was careful to not step above his station by out-dressing his betters. He had grey-green eyes that twinkled with intelligence but were wide with alarm as he looked at Julian, and more in particular his weapon and his readiness to use it.

Julian flinched as he recognized the building's landlord and took his hand away from his sword, clearing his throat in embarrassment.

At the other end of the room, Raedrick also had turned to face the entrance, but he stood calmly, his face passive and his arms still crossed over his chest. Bloody man and his unflappable nerve. It was sometimes quite annoying, though in all honesty Julian could remember a number of times when he had seen Raedrick unnerved.

"Master Lepolo," Raedrick said gravely, and inclined his head in greeting. His eyes flickered Julian's way and Julian thought he saw a little rebuke in his gaze.

The old man cleared his throat and returned Raedrick's nod with one of his own, though he kept a wary eye on Julian. "Constables. Just wanted to check who was up here, after..." He cleared his throat again, suddenly looking uncertain about something.

Raedrick frowned. "After what?"

Lepolo looked over his shoulder, down the stairs leading to the street below, and chewed on his lip for a second, as though considering how to answer. "Fellow came by here early this morning, asking to take a look at the event, as he called it. I told 'im to get the hell out, and he went. But when I saw the door open, I thought maybe he came back."

Julian felt his eyebrows climbing high onto his head. The only people who would have had any reason to come in here, besides Beverlee and Lepolo, were he and Raedrick. It was no one else's business, or at least the people in town new better - and were in general not inclined - than to butt in.

"Who was it?"

Lepolo shook his head. "Can't rightly say. Never seen 'im before today. Small fellow. Wiry. Black hair, dressed all fancy. Young. Carried a big ol' staff, which I thunk was odd 'cause he didn't have any trouble walking around." He gave a little shiver. "Seemed polite enough, but there was something about 'im..." He trailed off.

Julian met Raedrick's eyes and found that his friend's eyebrows were also riding high, though he had a grim expression on his face. Julian couldn't blame him. He knew who the landlord's visitor was, just as Julian did.

Julian sighed. Mages were such a hassle.

HOT PURSUIT

Tracking Loran down was harder than Julian thought it would be. He was not at The Oarlock. When asked, Molli shrugged and replied that he had gone to City Hall. But there was no sign of him there either. In fact, the clerks on duty had not seen him since his meeting with Mayor Brimly, the previous day.

That put Julian's hackles up. There seemed no reason to lie about where he was going. Not to his innkeeper, at least. What was Loran up to?

"He did say he was in town on Magestirium business," Raedrick said as they departed City Hall. "I know Melanie said not to worry, but..." He left the rest unsaid.

Julian could not stop the little icy ball of fear from forming in his belly.

He did not need to ask; neither of them did. With unspoken resolve, they turned left toward the outskirts of town, and Melanie's shop.

And found it locked up, closed for the day.

Julian stared at the shop door, and the little CLOSED sign hanging in the window, and that little ball of ice grew larger. He glanced up at the sun, about halfway down toward its resting place in the east. It was still relatively early in the afternoon, far to early to have ended business for the day, and Melanie was meticulous about her business. Where was she?

"I don't like this."

Raedrick nodded agreement.

"You don't think he's taken her?" Julian paused. "What does the Magestirium do when they catch..." He let the thought go.

"You know as much about their procedures as I do, Julian." Raedrick's tone was solemn, in that way he got when he was trying a little too hard to be comforting.

"So nothing, in other words." Julian turned on his heel and strode back toward Main Street. After a few strides, he realized he was more stalking than walking and forced himself to slow to a more normal pace, but it was tough. He felt as though he was about to jump out of his skin, anxious as he was becoming.

"I'm sure she's fine." Raedrick had to hurry to catch up, despite having the advantage of longer legs. "She's more than capable of - "

"You think I don't know that?" Julian winced inwardly at his own tone. He did not need to be snapping like that.

Raedrick did not reply, but walked at his side, his expression serious, focused.

They turned right onto Main Street and passed several crossing streets before Julian began to think about where he was leading them. Where would a Mage go who had captured an enemy of the Magestirium? Maybe to the local Constabulary? No, he would not trust them with this, or even the local judge. This was an internal Magestirium matter, and the Magestirium answered to the King but few others. Loran would bundle up his prisoner and get her out of sight, or just leave town immediately.

He had not departed yet, though. Julian was certain he would not leave his Inn bill unpaid. So there was still time to rescue Melanie. Maybe.

They passed City Hall and continued down Main Street. All around, the people went about their business with an air of wariness. Furtive glances down each side street and between buildings. People walking in clusters more than singly. Children who normally would have been allowed to roam freely kept within arm's reach of their mothers.

The town was on-edge, even more so than it had been this morning. In his own nervousness about Melanie, Julian had failed to notice it, but a patina of fear lay over everyone. The rumors must have spread, and in spreading multiplied as rumors do.

"And we don't have a clue, still," Julian muttered under his breath. He came to a halt. Raedrick stopped next to him, a questioning eyebrow quirked upward.

Julian sighed. "This isn't accomplishing anything," he said. "If he's taken her, we won't be able to get her back from him." It was like a knife in the gut, admitting that, but it was true. The only reason they had managed to overcome Isenholf's Mage ally was Melanie had lent her own skills to the fight. Without some form of magical backup, Loran would wipe the floor with them. "Maybe we should..."

He stopped speaking as a figure caught his eye down the street. Slender and small, in loose-fitting dark clothing that was almost a robe, the figure had dark skin and black hair, and bore a staff in his right hand. Loran. He was walking toward them from the edge of town, where Main Street became the dirt road leading to the old Rangers Station.

"Maybe we should go say hello," Raedrick said, not quite finishing Julian's original thought.

Julian nodded agreement. "Let's."

They met on the south side of Main Street, in front of a seamstress shop that was owned by a friend of Molli's, a pleasant, plump woman of advancing age who still had a mind as sharp as a tack, and a wit to match. Julian had more than once been moved to near tears over one of Poleen's stories, funny as they were. As he and Raedrick stopped in front of her shop, he could see her through the window, leaning over one of her apprentices as the younger girl worked. Correcting her stitching, no doubt.

Loran stopped a few paces in front of them, a vaguely amused smirk on his face. "Pleasant day, Constables," he said by way of greeting. It was, in fact, stifling. And humid. The back of Julian's shirt felt like it was going to be permanently stuck to his back by sweat, and he could really use a drink or six. Loran, however, looked as though he was not sweating at all. "To what do I owe the pleasure this time?"

"Why did you try to enter our crime scene this morning?" Raedrick asked without preamble.

Loran blinked twice, cocking his head to the side almost like a bird. For a second he almost looked surprised by the question. But that surely was not the case. He had to know Lepolo would have told them about his visit. Finally, he rolled his shoulders in a relaxed shrug and answered. "Mere curiosity. I've seen a number of murder scenes in the past, but only rarely one so gruesome as that."

Raedrick's eyes narrowed. "You went inside, after Master Lepolo told you to leave?" There was more than a hint of steel in his voice. He was clearly irritated.

Julian was right there with him.

Loran waved his free hand dismissively. "Hardly. But the events in that flat are the talk of the town. Or hadn't you heard?" A single eyebrow quirked upwards, mockingly. "Remarkably similar to how you found the man in the woods, hmm?"

Raedrick rested the palm of his left hand on his sword's pommel. "What are you about here, Magester Haversted?"

"As I said, just idle curiosity." Loran looked away from the two law men, his expression relaxed, almost bored. "If you will excuse me." Then he stepped to the side and around Raedrick and commenced to resume his walk down the street.

Raedrick turned with the Mage and watched him walk away, his expression stony.

"He's up to something," Julian said, "and I'll wager it's not good."

Raedrick frowned ever so slightly. "Perhaps." Then he straightened his shoulders and drew in a quick breath. Turning toward Julian, he grinned quickly. "At least we know he doesn't have Melanie. That's something."

Julian nodded, but could not quite return the grin. It *was* something. Not much, but something.

AN OATH BETRAYED

Baelin and Ilsa owned a small cottage on the west side of town off Cannery Street, not far from Julian's own flat as it turned out. Down a small intersecting street that more fit the term alley—as far as Julian knew it had no official name, it was just "That Alley Over There" to the locals—that ran between a pair of large boarding houses where the younger fishing men tended to live, the cottage, though small by any standards, had a certain charm to it. It was obvious that Baelin cared for their dwelling; the roof and shutters were in good repair and while the sides did not exactly gleam, they clearly had a fresh coating of paint done this summer. A well-ordered garden lay off to the cottage's left side, planted with all manner of vegetables and a couple of small trees - fruit bearing, Julian was sure. All told, the cottage was a home, well and true.

It seemed a shame to bring more trouble to this family's door.

Raedrick knocked on the front door, his expression stolid; he did not like being here either. But there were questions that needed answering.

The door cracked open a short moment later and a young boy looked out at them. Maybe seven years old, with dirty-blond hair and eyes that were red as though he had been crying—and why not?—he wore a rumpled off-white shirt and baggy brown pants, and no shoes.

"Deven," Raedrick said, recognizing the boy from Baelin's funeral, "is your mother home?"

Deven bit his lip and nodded quickly, then disappeared from view, leaving the door ajar. The sound of low conversation followed briefly, and then the door opened fully.

Ilsa was small and lean, with short-cut hair that was blond but these days going more to silver. She wore a simple light-blue dress with little white flowers at the hem and collar, and a white sash about her waist. She wiped her hands on a stained piece of cloth and looked that them with the expression of a person who had just sucked on a lemon.

"What do you want?" Her voice was strained, weary, to go along with her sunken eyes. She had not been getting much sleep these last few days, from the look of her.

"We don't mean to intrude - "

"Well you are." Ilsa began to push the door closed.

Raedrick stepped forward raising his hands in a mollifying gesture. "Please, Ilsa. We need to ask you some questions, in light of what's happened."

She scowled. "You weren't so keen on questions when it was just my Baelin. But now that that hussy died too, *now* you want to talk with me?" She snorted, then slammed the door in Raedrick's face.

Raedrick took a step back from the door, open confusion on his face. He looked at Julian and spread his hands helplessly. "What was that?"

Julian just shook his head, as stunned as Raedrick looked. He had never heard anyone in town say anything bad about Beverlee. At least not openly. There were the rumors, spoken in whispers behind her back, but they mostly dealt with speculation about why she seemed to have no interest in men at all. There was never any hint of implication that she was of low character.

"I don't know," Julian said. "It's almost like..." He trailed off as a thought struck him.

It was out of the question. Completely. And yet...

"What if..." He stopped, cleared his throat, then started again. "Molli told me that on the night Baelin died, Ilsa accused Helena of helping her sister fool around with him." He leaned a little closer to Raedrick and said, more softly, "What if that was more than just insecurity speaking?"

Raedrick's eyebrows climbed high on his head and his mouth dropped open for a second. Julian could see the wheel turning, though, and shortly he was all business again, his lips compressing into a grim scowl. "If Beverlee *were* seeing anyone, Helena would know."

Julian nodded. "She's holding out on us."

The sun was just half its own width above the mountains to Lydelton's east when Raedrick and Julian got to the little store-front that Helena and Beverlee had converted into their class-room. One building down from a leatherworking shop and across from a carpenter, it was not exactly the location Julian would necessarily have picked for a school. He would have thought of someplace more quiet, pristine. But then, the sisters' business was thriving, and had been for years, so they were doing something right. Who was Julian to criticize?

Helena was just closing up when they arrived, the children having long since gone back to their parents for the evening. As they approached, Julian watched her locking up the front door to their school with a mixture of admiration and confusion. He did not think he could have brought himself to do anything the day after his twin and best friend had been buried, let alone try to teach a bunch of demanding children.

Hell, he was surprised the parents sent them at all this day. But then, looking at the determined set of her face as Helena turned away from the door—it almost concealed the pain in her eyes. Almost—he would have given good odds she stalked over to each house herself to collect the kids for their lessons. That took some gumption.

Helena saw him and Raedrick approaching and offered them a quick, tired smile that almost, but not quite, reached her eyes. "Constables."

Julian returned her smile with one of his own. "Good evening, Helena," he said, as gently as he could.

Raedrick merely nodded politely in greeting.

They stood there in silence for a short while, just looking at each other. For his part, Julian was not sure how to bring it up all of a sudden. How do you ask a grieving woman if her twin had been engaging in adultery? He cleared his throat. "We need to ask you a...delicate...question."

Helena drew back slightly, her expression becoming guarded. Her eyes flicked between Julian and Raedrick, questioningly.

Julian drew a quick breath, then found he could not figure out how to say it -

"Was Beverlee in a relationship with Baelin?"

Julian recoiled almost as much as Helena did, the way Raedrick just threw it out there. He glanced aside at his friend. Raedrick wore the smallest of scowls, his brow furrowing in focused disapproval. Julian was a bit shocked; Raedrick was normally more politic than this.

Helena swallowed and wiped her hands along the front of her dress, black today, to reflect her grieving status. For that matter, why was Ilsa not dressed for mourning? Helena opened her mouth to speak, then shut it and lowered her eyes. Then, almost imperceptibly, she nodded.

"Tell us," Raedrick said.

Helena did not look up. If anything, she seemed to shrink back even further. "It started six months ago. Baelin helped her with a problem parent who had been harassing her. She..." Helena bit back a sob. "She had not been interested in men at all, not for years. Not since Ferdrik."

She wiped her nose on the back of her hand, like a little kid, and glanced up at them quickly. If she expected them to recognize the name, or see some significance in it, Julian did not know what it was.

After a moment, she began again. "Baelin must have heard about the harassment from one of the other men. He..." She shrugged. "Well, whatever he did, word got back to Beverlee, and she wanted to thank him. One thing led to another, and..." She trailed off, lowering her eyes back to the ground. "They met once or twice a week in his hideaway, somewhere out in the Glamorwood."

She was clearly conflicted. On the one hand, she had to be happy that her sister had found joy, if not love, in her life.

Not to mention sex.

On the other hand, Beverlee's actions were shameful, in the extreme. Julian was not sure how he would have reacted, if his brother had done the same.

Strange that he had not thought about his brother until just then. It had been how many months now, since he and Raedrick fled their unit in the Army? And how many months—hell, years —before that since he last saw Jered? He must be a full-grown man by now, laying waste to entire platoons of maidens, judging by the way the school girls used to swoon over his every smile.

Julian almost found himself chuckling over his brother's imagined antics, until he remembered where he was, who he was speaking to, and the circumstances. And even though he was more than halfway expecting it, the outright admission made Julian's stomach sink a bit. There was the answer, to both questions. Ilsa was not keeping with the normal mourning rituals because she was not truly mourning.

Ilsa was their killer.

❧ 13 ☙

COMPARING NOTES

"That doesn't make any sense." Raedrick snapped the words off quickly, but it sounded almost like he was trying to work himself through the notion more than he was trying to refute it. "How would Ilsa be able to do...that...to Beverlee, let alone to Baelin? She's not a big woman. I doubt she could lift an axe big enough to chop a body apart like that, let alone wield it effectively."

Julian had to admit, he had a point. Ilsa was the prime suspect, from circumstance and motive if for no other reason. But the method of the killings... That was troublesome. "Maybe she hired someone. Or she learned a little magic somewhere."

"What, like Melanie?" Raedrick shook his head and rested his palms on the top of his desk.

They were back in their office. After leaving Helena, they had walked back to the Constabulary, for lack of any better place to go as much as for the need to sit and think it through, and settled down into their respective seats. The brainstorming had gone downhill almost from the start.

"I truly doubt more than one Melanie will happen in any generation," Raedrick said, to complete his thought.

"Well, I should hope not."

Julian leapt out of his chair at the completely unexpected voice, which seemed to emanate from the air itself. Without thinking about it, he pulled his longsword from its scabbard and vaulted over his desk, landing on the balls of his feet in a ready stance.

Across the room from him, Raedrick had done similarly, except that he stood with most of his weight on his rear foot and he held his Tyrashi blade in both hands, with the sharp side of the blade pointing toward the ceiling and the hilt even with his right shoulder.

Julian had never seen such a ready stance before; where had Raedrick learned it?

Then he looked more closely at his friend and saw that his feet were positioned awkwardly, far enough apart that it would be difficult for him to move quickly, and his shoulders were very tense. It was almost like he was trying to force the stance, to merge himself into some form that he thought he should be taking. To match the sword?

From sparring him, Julian knew that Raedrick, despite months of training with his new blade, still was not comfortable with it. He still wanted to revert to the movements and forms he knew, and executed so well, from his old saber. His moves, though improved, were awkward, like he was fighting himself.

Before he accepted Selam's blade, Julian knew he would not have lasted a single pass in a duel with Raedrick. Now... Now, Raedrick was a shadow of his former self, at best Julian's equal, but by no means the master he once had been.

Raedrick flexed his fingers on the grip of his sword, his eyes glancing around the room nervously. How much of that nervousness came from his uncertainty with his weapon?

Julian looked around the room and scowled. There was no one else here, so where did...

Deep laughter emanated from out of nowhere, a vibrant chord that Julian recognized after a second or so. He should have known immediately who it was, but the shock of hearing that voice stopped his brain from working. He lowered his sword sheepishly and rose from his ready crouch.

"Dammit, Melanie!"

Her laughter only intensified as, off to Julian's left, in front of the cell block door, Melanie suddenly appeared in his view. She stood with her arms crossed over her breasts, shaking her head with a look of mocking amusement on her face. As always, she was dressed impeccably. Tonight, it was a deep burgundy dress and what Julian assumed was the same belt as before.

She smirked at the pair of them. "Honestly, boys, you are *far* too easy."

Julian sheathed his sword. He put an extra little zip into the process at the end; the steel of his blade's hilt struck the metal mouth of his scabbard with a fair-sounding CLACK, and all the while he just glared at Melanie. She returned the glare with a sardonic look of her own.

"What do you think you're doing?" Raedrick said sternly. He had also replaced his sword. He regarded her with his hands on his hips, looking for all the world like he was about ready to chew her a new one.

Melanie shrugged slightly and said, calmly, "Do calm down." She swayed over to one of the chairs that sat along the wall near the front door and settled down, taking a moment to smooth her skirts. "I thought we could compare notes."

Julian and Raedrick shared a look. The stern expression remained, but Raedrick looked puzzled now.

"I don't think so," Julian said. "We're still in the middle of our investigation and you're not..."

"Involved?" Melanie quirked an eyebrow archly. "You seemed to think I would become involved, the other day."

Julian rolled his eyes.

"Have you learned something that might help us find the killer?" Raedrick cut straight to the point, at least.

Melanie shrugged. "Maybe, but I doubt it." She crossed her

legs and leaned back in the chair. "Not unless Loran turns out to be the guilty party. I've been following his movements."

Raedrick lost his stern expression, his mouth instead falling open in surprise. Julian felt poleaxed, though of course thinking about it he really should not have been. Melanie had taken their warning and turned it on its head, taken the initiative to ferret out how much she needed to be concerned. That was laudable.

But still...

"That's a big risk," Julian said. "If he caught you..." He shook his head. "Better to just stay clear of him."

Melanie blew out a forceful snort that somehow managed to not seem at all un-ladylike. "So he can ambush me at a time and place of his choosing?" She shook her head with vigor. "I am quite capable of discretion, if you recall. Unless he were actively taking precautions against my techniques—and I assure you he did not —he would not notice if I were standing two feet from him."

Julian frowned as he thought that over. Melanie's concealment spells were potent, he knew that for true. They were perhaps *the* primary reason the town won out over Isenholf's brigands. But Loran was a mage as well, and from what hints Melanie had dropped probably much more skilled than she. Somehow Julian was not so certain he was as oblivious as she claimed, or hoped.

All the same, Loran had been acting strangely. Julian glanced over at Raedrick and shrugged his shoulders. The die was cast; might as well make use of the result.

Raedrick sighed again and nodded, then he settled back down into his desk chair. "Tell us."

"He has crisscrossed the town over the last couple days, and performed a number of detection rituals." She held up a fore-stalling hand at Julian, no doubt seeing the sudden flash of alarm that shot through him. "Not the sort that would have detected my spell. Something else." She frowned slightly, shaking her head. "I did not recognize the specifics of the ritual, just enough to know that it was meant to find something or someone. Who or why, I can only speculate upon. However," she leaned forward and looked meaningfully at both of them, "he went by Beverlee and Helena's house this morning, and was in the midst of setting up another ritual when their landlord chased him away."

Loran's presence at their flat was hardly surprising. The fact that he was preparing a spell, though...

"And then what?"

"Then," Melanie said. "Then, he walked into the woods past the Ranger Station to a clearing with a large boulder. The place you found Baelin, yes?"

Julian and Raedrick both nodded, soundlessly. Melanie returned the nod with a look of satisfaction.

"He performed his ritual again. This time he seemed quite a bit more excited, as though his results were different than at the other locations. Whatever he is looking for, I would wager it has something to do with your killings."

"We knew he went to Beverlee and Helena's. We bumped into him on the street, and he said it was just idle curiosity."

Melanie smirked at Julian's words and gave a little shake of her head. "Loran Haversted does not engage in idle curiosity. There is a purpose to his every action."

Raedrick looked levelly at Melanie for a moment before speaking slowly, his tone chilly. "You didn't tell us you knew him."

"You did not ask, did you?"

Raedrick just looked at her, accusation in his eyes. Finally, after what seemed a much longer moment than it probably was, she rolled her eyes and raised her hands in supplication.

"Fine. Fine, I know him. Or rather, I know *of* him, and I am very glad that he does not know me." Her expression darkened, something like pain or...fear?...flashing across her face before she schooled herself to calm. "You recall the hypothetical mage we discussed when we first met?"

How could they forget? It had not taken long for Julian to puzzle out that Melanie was a mage, and bugger the restrictions against women studying at the Magestirium. One five-minute conversation, really. And when it became clear how overmatched the town was against Isenholf's brigands, he and Raedrick had sought her out for support. She had alluded to the possibility of a hypothetical mage and a hypothetical woman falling in love and him sharing the Magestirium's secrets with her, but she had not elaborated.

"I remember. Timon, you said his name was," Julian said, with no small amount of apprehension. For some reason he was not sure he wanted to hear this part of her story.

Melanie nodded and flashed the barest hint of an approving smile before replying. "Loran is a Vigilant—one of the Magestirium's Inquisitors."

"Inquisitors? I haven't heard of them before," Raedrick said, one eyebrow quirking upward.

"And you would not have. They are the Magestirium's internal police force, and rarely interact with the uninitiated on official business." That little smile faded into a scowl. "Vigilant Haversted was the one who led the investigation into Timon's...impropriety." She shuddered visibly and looked away from them, off into space. "I do not know how long they tortured him before the end, but I do know he did not betray his secrets, at least not the ones he kept closest to his heart."

"How do you know that?"

Melanie gave Julian a direct look, one filled with suppressed pain that was eclipsed by a deep and abiding anger. "Because I am still alive." Her lips compressed for a moment and then, with the brush of her hand through her hair, the deep emotions were gone, replaced by her normal slightly sardonic half-smile. "So." She clasped her hands together and leaned forward slightly. "Ilsa?" She shook her head. "She's not the murdering type."

Julian had to do a double-take, quick as her demeanor changed. Glancing over at Raedrick, he got a cocked eyebrow in return, followed by a quick shrug of the shoulders before Raedrick answered.

"You knew her well?"

Melanie shook her head again. "Not really. She came into the shop once or twice, looking for home remedies. Although," she frowned slightly and tapped the tip of her index finger against her lips as she paused, considering her words for a moment, "a couple weeks ago she alluded to having a more difficult problem she might need help with, but it never went any further than that."

"An unfaithful husband *is* a difficult problem," Julian said.

Melanie shrugged slightly. "Don't know what she would have expected me to do about that. No, more likely it was one of the children. Runny bowels for an excessive duration, or something."

Julian coughed into his hand; that was not the direction he wanted the conversation to turn. Melanie shot him an amused glance.

"So Baelin was cheating and she killed him for it. And Beverlee as well?" She shook her head again, her face doubtful. "I don't see it."

"We know he was unfaithful," Raedrick said.

"Do you?"

He exchanged a semi-confused look with Julian. "Helena said so, and Ilsa more than implied it."

Melanie spread her hands as though to say, "If you say so," but she still looked doubtful. Either about the infidelity or the murder plot.

Or both.

And Julian had to admit she had a point. All they had was implication from the wife and hearsay from the sister. Though why would Beverlee lie to Helena about that? But that would not be enough to bring before the judge. If they had some proof...

"Helena said Baelin had some sort of hideaway out in the woods, and that's where they met." Julian looked over at Raedrick and leaned forward. "Maybe there's something there that can shed some more light on what was going on."

Raedrick frowned, chewing at his lip for a moment, then he nodded. "True. But do you have the first idea where to look for it?"

"No." Before heading out to the site of Baelin's murder, Julian had never set foot in the Glamorwood. He would not have a clue where anyone... But then, he did not have to. "But I think I know who would."

BOOZE AND BLOOD

Julian expected Melanie to make more of a fuss, so he was surprised when her only response to his suggestion that she not accompany he and Raedrick was to arch an eyebrow at him and say, "Of course."

He just stared at her in silence for a moment. He had carefully prepared arguments ready to use about how it would be best if she were not visibly associated with this case, since Loran was apparently so interested in it. And maybe she should keep up the disappearing trick she pulled the last couple days, just in case. But with her ready agreement, the arguments all fell out from the bottom of his brain.

Melanie stood and walked toward the door, shaking her head slightly. "It's better if I not stick my neck out. Loran does not appear to be looking for me after all, but that doesn't mean I should bring attention to myself."

And then she left their office.

As the door swung shut behind her, Raedrick said, "Well. That was easy." He sounded as surprised as Julian felt.

"Yeah."

Raedrick stood up. "Where are we going then?"

"I figure if anyone knows where Baelin's hideout is, Dewey

does." Julian took a moment to adjust his swordbelt, then set out for the door. "I heard him saying he was going for a drink at Holb's Tavern after Baelin's funeral. Could be they'll know where to find him there."

Raedrick blanched visibly.

Holb's Tavern was similar to The Oarlock in that they both served ale. Aside from that, though...

While The Oarlock was really an Inn with a spacious taproom and well-run kitchens, Holb's was almost literally a hole in a wall. The building it resided in was at one point in time an armory, or so some of the oldsters in Lydelton told Julian. Sitting on the western edge of town, a block and a half from the last of the finger-piers that jutted into Lake Glimmermere, the building was squat, long, and narrow, painted a deep red that was nearly black, and steadily falling past ill-kept toward dilapidated. Down near the end of the building farthest from the center of town, a twenty foot section of the outer wall had been removed and a wide awning installed that extended a good thirty feet out from the side of the building. The bar took up the entire length of the building where the wall used to be, and the serving area was a paved expanse beneath the awning. That awning served as the tavern's main shelter from the elements. Julian would have thought Holb would close up shop when it got cold because of that, but apparently he had canvas sides that laced in place around the awning. Those combined with braziers inside made the tavern pleasantly warm. Supposedly.

"I can't believe so many people frequent this place," Raedrick said as the two of them came to a halt in front of the old armory.

Indeed, a fair-sized crowd was already gathered, in spite of the relatively early hour; it was just getting toward dinner time, and Holb's did not serve food, only drink. About two dozen men, and a few women as well, mostly fishing men and laborers of other stripes from the look of them, drank and laughed in the serving area. Though their laughter was a bit less raucous than usual and several of the faces in the crowd had a strained look that even the flush of drink could not mellow.

Even here, there was fear.

Julian smirked at Raedrick's remark. "It can be an entertaining place."

Raedrick just snorted, a look of distaste on his face. Apparently he still felt the sting from his last visit.

Julian led the way into the serving area, slipping past a group of men who were crowded around a table where a pair of particularly burly fellows were engaged in an arm-wrestling contest. They were quite enthusiastic in cheering on their favored contestant, and from the way the men's arms were shaking it looked like they had been at it for a while. Julian chuckled and turned away. A moment later, groans of chagrin mixed with cheers of triumph as the contest ended.

Julian strode up to the bar and smacked his hand down flat on it.

The bar was not polished or stained. It was bare wood, pine he presumed though he could not tell from looking at it, and sanded to a smooth texture. Stains from multiple mugs and glasses and crude—and rude—drawings and writings of all sorts marred its surface, giving it a strangely homey look.

The man behind the bar was anything but.

Tall, with shoulders that dwarfed those of the bulkiest man in the tavern, he had a square face that seemed locked into a sour expression behind a thick black beard. Julian supposed his hair would have matched his beard, if he had any. But his head was completely bald, as though he shaved it regularly instead of his face. He had dark brown eyes that twinkled with intelligence, and irritation, and wore a stained white apron over a light blue, almost grey, shirt and black pants. A puckered scar crossed his forehead from just over his left eyebrow to his left ear, and that ear had a little notch cut out of it.

Julian had never heard how Holb got that scar. The one time he asked Holb about it, he received only a sour grunt in response, and no more drink that evening.

Holb scowled a greeting at Julian, but when his eyes moved from Julian to Raedrick the scowl became a near-feral growl, complete with baring of teeth.

"Whoa. Take it easy, Holb," Julian said, quickly. "We come in peace." He looked back at Raedrick, who was returning the hostile look in kind, and amended, "He comes in peace." He looked back at Holb and put on a winning grin, raising his hands in a gesture that he hoped was placating. "Just have a couple questions."

For a few seconds, Holb just stared daggers at Raedrick. The area became hushed, as the patrons around them sensed the tension between the two men. The silence grew quickly until it encompassed the entire serving area. Everyone —Julian did not stop to look but he was absolutely certain everyone in the area— was staring at them in hushed anticipation.

The last time Raedrick came here, he had somehow managed to insult Holb's wife. Julian had no idea how; he had never seen Raedrick behave except chivalrously. But somehow he managed it, and Holb had personally come over the bar and thrown Raedrick out of his place. Julian had not seen it, but rumors were Holb did it with embarrassing ease. Whatever the truth of the incident was, and he never spoke of it, Raedrick had moved rather stiffly for the next few days, and he had never returned to Holb's Tavern.

Julian fervently hoped there was not going to be a repeat this evening.

Finally, Holb nodded, ever so slightly. He snorted Raedrick's way then turned his full attention on Julian.

Softly, almost imperceptibly, it seemed the entire population of customers and serving girls let out a breath they had all been holding. Julian found that he did the same.

He cleared his throat and put his smile back on. "Two pints of ale please, Holb." Holb's scowl intensified again. "Ok, just one."

He waited until the barkeep brought his drink, then plunked down payment and took a swig before speaking again. "Have you seen Dewey around?"

Holb cocked his head to one side and his bushy eyebrows rose slightly. "What ya want wit him?"

Julian took another drink and paused, looking down at the mug. It was good. Damn good. "You using a new formula?"

Holb shrugged ever so slightly and grunted in reply. Julian could not be sure, but it almost looked like he might have slightly smiled for a second. "Just 'xperimenting."

"Well that's pretty damn tasty."

Holb's head dipped ever so slightly in acknowledgement. His brow furrowed a bit. Get to the point, Constable.

"Right." Julian took another sip. "We need to ask Dewey a few questions about Baelin. Part of the investigation."

Holb's brow furrowed even more and his scowl deepened.

"He's not in trouble or anything. We thought he could help us out, is all."

The big barkeep glowered for a long, silent moment. Then he shrugged and turned away. He walked over to where one of his serving girls waited, then proceeded to fill several mugs from one of the kegs behind the bar. He placed them on her tray, and she departed.

Julian could not help but follow her with his eyes. Holb's girls always wore the most appealing outfits. Tight in just the right areas, but not so much as to do more than tease. It made for a good sight.

Holb's big beefy hand slapped down on the bar next to Julian, and he jumped ever so slightly as he turned to look back at the big bartender. "Bigsbe's," said Holb.

Julian nodded. "Thanks."

Holb just grunted.

Bigsbe's Boarding House lay on the north side of town, only two blocks away from Julian and Raedrick's office. Two stories tall, it boasted twelve small rooms on the upper level, a small common area on the ground floor that held a couple bookshelves, a quartet of chairs, and a small writing desk, and a common bath house and privy in the rear. Julian had visited the place on two previous occasions, to mediate minor squabbles between a few of the tenants, and found it relatively clean and well-cared-for, as boarding houses went.

Madaleen Bigsbe, the proprietress, held court from a small office near the front of the common area. But when Julian and Raedrick walked in the stout wooden double-doors at the front of the building, she was nowhere to be seen. Small wonder, concerning the hour. She had family to attend to, after all.

"Isn't there a night attendant?"

Julian sniffed in amusement at Raedrick's words and almost voiced a bitingly sarcastic riposte, but looking at him, he was still perturbed from their interaction with Holb. So Julian let it lie. Mostly. "It's not an Inn, Rae."

"I know that. But if she's going to leave the place unlocked, someone ought to keep an eye out. Keep thieves from making off with her books, if nothing else."

Fair point. Julian shrugged and poked his head into the little office. It was just large enough to contain a stout wooden desk and chair, a trio of narrow cabinets that Madaleen used for storing files, and a strongbox. The chair was pulled back from the desk as though someone had gotten up from it quickly. Adding to that impression, a cup of dark fluid, tea probably, sat on the blotter. Steam was still rising from the cup, and some of the tea had splashed out onto the blotter.

Julian frowned. "Looks like they left in a hurry." He looked back at Raedrick.

His friend returned his frown and loosened his sword in its sheath. "Something's not right here. Look sharp."

They separated by a few paces and advanced through the

common room to the passageway leading toward the bath house. Just outside the common room, on the left, a narrow set of stairs led up to the level above. Raedrick took the stairs two at a time, and Julian followed, a gnawing sense of dread in his gut that got more pronounced by the second.

The stairs ended at a small landing, then bent back on themselves before reaching the doorway to the second floor. They had just reached the landing when the soft sound, like a groan, reached Julian's ears.

He froze, drawing his sword and waiting, listening, for another sign. After a dozen or so seconds of silence, he glanced at Raedrick, who wore a mask of grim focus. Then another sound: breaking glass. Their eyes met, and Julian saw the same resolve, and dread, as he felt himself.

Not again.

The two men burst into the second floor corridor and looked quickly left and right. The stairs lay in the center of the building; in either direction were three pairs of doors, across the corridor from each other. Small oil lamps in wall sconces provided illumination that was just a bit better than twilight. But that was enough to see a figure lying prone near the farthest pair of doors to the left.

"Son of a bitch," Julian said as he sprinted down the corridor to the downed figure, Raedrick at his side.

They pulled up short and saw immediately that the prostrate person was dead. Her—and it was a she, a once very-pretty she too—head was twisted completely around so her glazed, lifeless eyes looked up at the ceiling despite the fact that her body lay on its belly.

"Son of a bitch," Julian repeated, more loudly, and squatted down next to the dead girl.

"Julian."

He looked up at Raedrick, and his friend nodded at the right-hand side door. It lay a couple inches ajar, and a cold breeze wafted into the hallway, carrying an unmistakable and recognizable stench. Julian's blood, already cold from finding the body, went like icy water, and that sense of dread returned threefold.

The scene inside the room was every bit as bad as Julian feared. And every bit the same as before.

The room was maybe ten feet square, with room for a bed and a desk and a small cabinet. The entire room was covered in blood, from the floor to the ceiling. Body parts were strewn everywhere, but mostly lay on the bed. As before, it was difficult to tell which part was which. Except for the head, resting atop the cabinet and staring at the scene in abject horror. Julian recognized Dewey's face immediately.

The room's lone window was shattered, only a few shards of glass still remaining in its pane. The drapes wafted in the chilly nighttime breeze lazily. For a moment Julian found himself focusing on that motion to the exception of everything else; a single point of normalcy in the insanity of the scene.

And then Raedrick was past him and peering about through the window. He hissed.

Julian hurried over and looked down. It took a short while to make out anything in the darkness.

"There."

Julian followed his friend's outstretched finger and squinted. There was nothing...

Wait. In the shadows between two adjacent buildings, something was moving. Hurrying away from Bigsbe's, but not running; that would draw attention. The figure kept to the shadows, moving furtively, until it reached the street.

It turned left and vanished from sight, but just before that happened, the light from a streetlamp cast details on the figure. Short, with dark hair and wearing dark robes. And carrying a large staff.

Julian felt his eyes growing wide.

❧ 15 ❧

UNDER ARREST

They ran to The Oarlock.

Raedrick had longer legs, and Julian had to push hard to match his pace, By the time they reached the Inn, he was out of breath and his legs felt rubbery. He did not normally run so far so quickly.

He derived some comfort from the fact that Raedrick was also breathing heavily. Some.

They burst into the taproom and veered straight toward the bar, where Molli held court. Julian hardly noticed the patrons except to think mildly that it was nice how they all got out of their way.

Respect.

No, wait. That wasn't it. They all looked startled, frightened. One serving girl squeaked as they rushed past and dropped her tray, and its contents, to the floor.

Molli watched this and scowled, planting her hands on her hips. "Stop right there!" Her voice cut through the air like a horn, bringing Julian up short, and Readrick with him. He had not heard someone shout like that, since...

All at once, he realized he still had his sword brandished. And...

He looked down at himself. His clothing was bloodstained in many places, from the scene in Dewey's room. Raedrick was in a similar state, and wore an murderous expression to go with it.

No wonder people had cleared out of their way. He and Raedrick must have scared the hell out of them.

Stupid.

"What do you think you're doing, charging in here like this?" Julian had seen Molli irritated before, but never truly angry. Until now. Her brow furrowed, her face flushed deep red, and her eyes glittered dangerously. "You get yourselves - "

Her tirade vanished beneath Raedrick's shouted, "Quiet!" His tone was the same whip-crack of command that he used during the heat of battle to order his squad to change tactics. He must have practiced it for weeks, because it was unerringly able to pierce the din of battle or, in this case, Molli's speech. Raedrick fixed a deadly serious stare on her, and she shrank back. "Loran Haversted," Raedrick continued in that same tone of command. "Where is he?"

All around, patrons looked at each other, Raedrick's words having easily reached their ears. Already he could see the wheels turning, the seeds of new rumors beginning to flourish.

Molli blinked, taken aback but obviously still angry. "His room, I think. What is this about? You have no right - "

"Which room?" Raedrick waited a half-second, then demanded again, more loudly. "Which room?"

"Room Seven. What - ?"

"The key."

Molli drew herself up and shook her head. "Now see here. You can't just barge into one of my guests' rooms. I've got a - "

"The key, or I break down the door."

Silence followed for several seconds and Molli and Raedrick locked eyes, her seething anger mixed with no little confusion against his rock-solid resolve. Slowly, Molli's expression changed, moving away from anger toward nervousness and then fear. She swallowed.

"He's not the one who..." She trailed off, her words lowering to a whisper as the import of what was happening sunk in.

"Just give us the key, Molli, so we can handle it."

Molli nodded shakily and reached into one of the pockets in her apron. She pulled out a medium-sized key ring and took a moment to fumble through them until she found the one she needed. She had to try twice to get it off the ring, and then she held it out to Raedrick.

"Thank you," he said, and snatched it out of her grasp. Then he turned toward the staircase at the rear of the taproom, glancing at Julian as he went. "Let's go."

Raedrick led the way up the stairs, with Julian right behind him.

It had been some time since he had last been on the Oarlock's upper level, and as they burst onto the upstairs landing, memories swept back over Julian. Good times, and bad. Mostly stressful, to be honest; they lived here during the conflict with Isenholf, and that was as stomach-clenching a situation as Julian had seen. Up until now, anyway.

He shoved the memories aside and followed his friend down the hall and around the corner to Room Seven. It was conveniently located adjacent to the baths and privy, but Julian was surprised that Loran had not opted for Molli's more luxurious suite. He certainly had the coin for it. Not that it mattered now.

They reached the door and paused for only the briefest of moments. Then Raedrick jabbed the key into the lock and shoved the door open.

The room was small, smaller than the room at Bigsbe's, but well furnished. It differed from the room Julian and Raedrick had stayed in in that there was only one bed, but aside from that it was identical.

Except that this room had a short mage with one leg out of the window, looking like he was just returning from some bit of malfeasance or another.

"Well," Julian said, "that answers that."

"How dare you?" Loran snapped, wrenching his leg over the window sill even as he reached for his staff, which lay on the floor, where he had dropped it while climbing in. "What is the meaning of this?"

Raedrick wasted no time in answering. Moving with all the speed at his disposal, and he had quite a lot, he bounded across the room and struck Loran with a left cross.

The mage did not even try to block it, so surprised he was. Raedrick's fist struck him in the cheek, and his head snapped backwards and to his left. He staggered backwards and struck the wall, then fell forward onto his knees as his hands flew to his face.

Raedrick grabbed him by the back of the neck and flung him to the ground, then straddled him as he took hold of his wrists and forced his hands behind his back. Then Raedrick looked up at Julian and quirked an eyebrow at him. Julian smirked and reached into the belt pouch where he kept his manacles, then handed them to him.

"Loran Haversted," Raedrick said in his most professionally cold tone while he locked the manacles around the mage's wrists. "You are under arrest for the murders of Baelin Rorickson, Beverlee Winslow, Cora Frederlan, and Dewey the woodsman."

"Preposterous," Loran said. "I demand you release me at once!"

Raedrick just snorted in his ear then, with Julian's help, hauled him to this feet.

Loran's right cheek was already beginning to swell. It was going to be one hell of a bruise. He was lucky Raedrick had not struck him lower, or he would have lost several teeth. All the same, his eyes were defiant, furious. "You are making a grave mistake, Constables." His voice was cold, venomous, promising swift retribution against them.

The problem was, Julian was not sure that he could not deal

out that retribution, even from a jail cell. From the look in his eyes, Loran believed he could do just that.

Julian just hoped they were right about this.

The journey from The Oarlock to the Constabulary was normally fairly quick, but this night it seemed to take forever. Halfway there, Loran seemed to come out of a daze and began to struggle surprisingly vigorously for a man his size, especially one who presumably did not get much in the way of exercise—after all, what need does a Mage have for physical force? It took both Julian's and Raedrick's full effort to keep him in line and going the right direction.

By the time they reached their office and got the cell block door open, though, it seemed to get through Loran's head that he was stuck and they were not going to let up. He ceased his struggles and complied with Raedrick's commands without complaint, even walking himself into his cell.

When they closed and locked the cell door, he wore a mocking little grin on his face that never translated to his eyes. They burned with simmering anger. Julian had been stared down by many men before, but he could not recall anyone off-hand who had done it as effectively as this Mage.

He hurried out of the cell block as quickly as he could once the cell was secured. He thought he heard Loran chuckle mockingly as he went.

✢ 16 ✢

A NOT-SO-FRIENDLY CHAT

The two of them divided their efforts. After getting Loran secured in his cell, Raedrick went back to Bigsbe's to more thoroughly investigate the scene, while Julian went back to The Oarlock to look through Loran's effects. Julian did not envy Raedrick his half of the night's investigation. Not one bit. But after an hour and a half in Loran's room with nothing of pertinence to show for it, he almost could have considered swapping.

Almost.

Finally, he decided to call it quits, and went back to the office.

Word had spread quickly about the arrest, or so it seemed. The streets were more crowded than normal for the hour—it was approaching four bells, bedtime for most—especially on a work night. But tonight groups of men turned to watch him pass at every street corner. A few shouted inquiries at him. Had they truly caught the killer? Was it safe for their wives to go out again? What about the children?

When was the hanging?

That came the most often, making Julian swallow nervously as he answered with only a shake of his head. If people got it into their heads that a hanging was in order, they might not be satisfied with anything short of that very thing. And if that became the case and they decided to take things into their own collective hands...

That could get ugly real quick.

Julian picked up his pace, hurrying his pace, but not enough to make it seem he was doing anything but walking. It was almost with a feeling of relief that he turned the last corner and caught sight of the Constabulary.

The feeling passed quickly as he beheld the scene there.

Mayor Brimly stood with Raedrick on the front porch outside of Julian and Raedrick's office. The Mayor was barely dressed. His leggings were clearly pajama pants that had been tucked hurriedly into his boots, and Julian could swear beneath his formal coat was only a pajama top. He wore his mayoral badge prominently though, and despite his disheveled appearance he did a fairly decent approximation of a man with power who was Lording over his subordinates.

Too bad Julian had seen him cower in the face of danger, not so very long ago, or he might have believed the act.

Mayor Brimly wrung his hands anxiously as Julian stepped up onto the porch, but the look he directed at Raedrick was made of steel. "What do you think you're doing?"

Raedrick was far more politic than Julian would have been. "Master Mayor, we caught him red handed, sneaking through the window of The Oarlock after we observed him fleeing the scene of tonight's murder. There can be no doubt."

Mayor Brimly began chewing on his lip for a moment, still wringing his hands while he pondered. Then, finally, he sighed, his shoulders slumping. "Do you have any idea what the Magestirium will do when they hear of this? It simply is not done, accosting a high-ranking member of their order like this."

"How many high-ranking members of their order engage in capital crimes, Master Mayor?" Julian could not keep the scorn from his voice. And why not? Any group that would blindly defend their own even when in the wrong was deserving of such.

Mayor Brimly glanced over at Julian and his scowl grew more dark. Then after a minute he nodded, conceding the point. "I still don't like it. We'll pay for this, mark me."

"But you agree we may proceed?"

Mayor Brimly inhaled and for a moment Julian thought sure he was going to say no. But then he let his breath out in a long sigh and nodded.

Raedrick returned the nod and pulled the Constabulary doors open, then disappeared within. Julian paused to make a quick half-bow, as befitted the Mayor's rank and position, then followed his friend.

Julian followed Raedrick into the cell block and tried not to shrink back from nerves. Mages were dangerous. Yes, they had taken away Loran's staff and anything that looked like it could be used as a component in some spell, but that did not mean Loran could not have other tricks up his sleeve.

The Mage was ensconced in the last cell on the left, as far from the barred doorway into the front office as possible. Very little light from the cell block's two lamps made it back into the cell, and for a moment it almost looked as though Loran was not there at all. Then a soft rustling issued from the cell and the shadows in the rear of the cell moved as Loran sat up from where he was lying on his little cot.

"I trust you have not come to set me free."

Julian snorted loudly and crossed his arms over his chest.

"Why did you kill them?" Raedrick's voice was cold, his expression sharp and focused, the way it got before a fight.

Julian's eyes had adjusted better to the dimness. He could just make out the outlines of Loran's face as he shook his head. "I have killed no one. Here."

"So it was just a coincidence that you were at the scene of tonight's murder." Raedrick sniffed slightly.

"Only the simplest of minds believes in such a thing as coincidence." Loran added an extra emphasis, and bit of derision to the last word.

Julian and Raedrick shared glances. That was not a denial. It also was not an admission.

"Alright," Raedrick said, "Why were you there, if you didn't do it?"

"Why were *you*, Constable?"

This was getting nowhere. "We're asking the questions here," Julian said, irritation lending extra heat to his tone that he had not intended. "If you don't want to never see the outside of a jail cell again, you'll - "

Loran chuckled, a soft sound that carried easily to Julian's ears and contained entire levels of disdain. "I do not answer to a man who lowers himself to the use of double negatives. And I will remain in this cell only as long as I deign to allow it. And not one second more." The shadow of his head shook and his body shifted, lying back down onto his cot. "Now leave me."

Julian ground his teeth to stop himself from lashing out with all manner of curses against the mage's lineage, particularly his mother. He had no idea what Loran was talking about, but he could deal with that. What really got under his skin was the superior attitude, the condescension, especially now while he was locked up. Did he not understand the situation, or was he arrogant enough to truly think little things like the law did not apply to him?

Probably the latter, if truth be told. The Magestirium had a nearly free hand in most things, answering only to the King. Only a couple of ignorant bumpkins would dare lay hands on one of their Order, let alone a member with the rank Loran apparently held.

Lord, but he hated being called bumpkin. Even when it was he who was doing the calling.

"You didn't answer the question, Loran," Raedrick said softly.

His eyes seemed to burn, reflecting the dim lamp light as though the lamp's fire was their own.

"But I have, Constable. You simply refuse to hear it." The shadow that was Loran moved slightly, making a mockingly dismissive gesture at them unless Julian missed his guess.

Then he lay still.

A moment later, soft snoring issued from the cell. How in the hell had he gotten to sleep that quickly, and with the pair of them standing right there, no less?

Julian shook his head and stalked toward the front office. He looked back as he stepped through the doorway. Raedrick was still there, staring daggers into the cell. He remained for almost a full minute before turning away and moving to join Julian.

Yes, this was not going well at all.

Raedrick closed the door to the cell block and locked it, then replaced the key on its ring near his desk. "What do you make of that?" he said.

"Arrogant cuss."

Raedrick snorted out a half-chuckle. "Did you expect anything else?" He flopped down into his desk chair and leaned back, chewing on his lip in thought.

"We could always yank off a fingernail or two," Julian offered as he took his own seat. "That'll help ease his tongue." He meant it as a bad joke, but the look Raedrick shot him stopped Julian cold. He raised his hands at the simmering anger in his friend's eyes. "Joke, Rae."

Raedrick scowled. "It's not funny."

"Yeah I can see that." So much for a little levity. "Well let's review. We've got him dead to rights at the scene, but we need more before he goes to the Judge." Julian held up a finger. "No blood on him. No sign he's been in a fight. Ever. No - "

"Only a mage could have killed those men the way they were, and a mage could easily clean himself up."

Julian nodded. "Yes, but do you think that will satisfy the judge? Did you find anything more definitive at the scene tonight"

Raedrick sighed and looked down at his desk. The simmering anger was gone, replaced by frustrated acceptance as he shook his head.

"I don't think so either."

"Any ideas?" Raedrick did not sound particularly hopeful.

Julian could not blame him. Maybe things would look better in the morning.

❧ 17 ❧

MISCALCULATION

They did not.

Julian and Raedrick met at their office just before dawn, with the intent to get back to questioning Loran again as soon as he woke. Maybe the initial disorientation of waking would shake loose some of the obstinance and get him to reveal something more.

Should have known better.

After a fruitless half hour, during which the only thing they managed to accomplish was establishing that the jail rations were not up to Loran's exacting standards, they left the cell block with no more answers than they had to begin with.

"Maybe we're - " Julian began.

Raedrick raised a finger to his lips and nodded toward the cell block door. Julian shut his mouth; his words would carry to Loran's ears easily through the bars. He followed Raedrick out to the front porch and closed the door, then began again.

"Maybe we're going about this wrong."

Raedrick quirked an eyebrow at him. "You think he's innocent?"

Julian shrugged. "Didn't say that."

"But you have doubts."

Julian spread his hands helplessly.

Raedrick nodded. "Me too." He sighed and looked away, toward the intersection with Main Street. "Dammit. We acted too soon, didn't we?"

"Hardly a surprise."

Melanie's voice, so unexpected right then, made Julian jump. He spun around and found her sitting on one of the paired chairs at the far end of the porch. He had not noticed her there when they came out.

Raedrick was similarly surprised. He spluttered for a half-second. "Melanie! What - " He stopped and glanced toward the office door, as though checking to make sure it was still closed. "What are you doing here?" he finished, in a more quiet tone.

She smiled slightly and ran her hands down her legs, smoothing her dress. It was dark green today, laced in yellow-gold near the hems. "Checking up on you, of course. When I heard what happened last night..." Her smiled grew more broad. "I would have loved to have been there to see you hit him."

Julian did not have to work hard to keep from smiling in return. "You know something, don't you? Why don't you just spit it out?"

Melanie's smile faded a bit. She pushed a lock of her hair back over her ear and shrugged. "I know a lot of things. But as to Loran's guilt for the murders..." She shrugged. "I'd like to think he's guilty so he can get his just deserts. But I don't see *why* he would have done it. What's the gain?"

"Some people don't need to see any gain to kill someone. The killing *is* the gain to them."

Melanie frowned slightly, then inclined her head, conceding Julian's point.

"But he is too smart for that," Raedrick said. "If he were the bloodthirsty type, he would at least do it in a manner that he wouldn't be caught. Killing in a way that only a mage could... It's too simple to pin it on him."

Julian was forced to concede that. "That tracks."

"So why do you have him locked up in your cell block?" Melanie threw her hands up and rose from her chair, shaking her head with a mixture of bemusement and exasperation. She strode past them and descended the stairs to the street, still shaking her head.

"Honestly, you two," she looked over her shoulder at them and did not even try to keep the snark from her voice. She would have fit in nicely in the Magestirium, if only they allowed women. "You truly are incredible." She did not make that sound good at all.

She strode away in that half-sashay she used when she walked that made her hips sway oh so enticingly. Julian could not help but watch until she disappeared from view around the corner to Main Street.

"She's right, you know."

Julian nodded. "We've stepped in it this time. Mayor's going to have our heads. Assuming Loran leaves anything left for him."

Raedrick sighed. He ran his hand through his hair and just looked out at the street, almost empty of traffic at this still early hour. Finally, he said, "Let's set him loose."

❧ 18 ❧

TRADING SECRETS

L oran sat in front of Raedrick's desk and looked at him with coldly contemptuous eyes. The dark scowl on his lips made grim counterpoint to the swollen bruise that dominated his right cheek. That must have pained him something fierce, but he had made no complaint and it did not seem to phase him at all as he spoke.

"Well?"

Julian, standing to Raedrick's right, looked away from the mage, toward the front door of their office, and for a moment almost hoped that someone would come in. Like the Mayor maybe.

Now that was a stupid thought.

"I...apologize," Raedrick said, "for how we behaved toward you, Magester Haversted." He cleared his throat and lowered his eyes toward the top of his desk for a moment. Then he took a deep breath and forced himself to meet the Mage's gaze once more. "We jumped to conclusions. I have no excuse."

Loran kept his eyes locked on Raedrick's for several seconds. Then he sniffed and looked toward Julian. As his eyes met the Mage's, Julian felt his blood run cold. There was deadly menace there. The promise of retribution to come that no force in the world could prevent. He tried to swallow, but his mouth had suddenly gone dry.

"And you?"

Julian inclined his head, the way a man did when conceding defeat in the sparring ring. "Sincere apologies, Magester."

Loran waited for a half-minute, then gave the quickest of nods. "I accept your apology." He flashed a smile that oozed condescension. "You are dealing with forces beyond your understanding and comprehension. You can be forgiven for being...abrupt."

Julian ground his teeth to keep himself from voicing a retort in keeping with the Mage's condescension. Fun as that would have been, it really would not do, not after he and Raedrick had put their feet into it so deeply with him.

Silence loomed for another half-minute. Then Loran stood and pulled his shirt - it was more a tunic than a shirt, truth be told - straight. He picked up his staff, which lay propped against the office wall, and the satchel which contained his other goods. "Good day, gentlemen," he said, and turned toward the door.

"Wait."

Loran stopped, looking back at Raedrick with a quirked eyebrow.

"You know something, Magester," Raedrick said. "Something about what's been going on here. The murders."

A smirk was the Mage's only response.

Raedrick rolled his eyes. "Dammit, people are dying. *Our* people, and we are the ones who are supposed to keep them safe. And the only thing we can tell is they were killed with magic. If you know something, tell us." He paused, then drew a deep breath and added, "Please."

That had to hurt. It made Julian's stomach lurch just hearing his friend all but beg from this man. But Raedrick was right. It had to be a Mage committing these murders. And if it was not Loran, and it certainly was not Melanie, that left the two of them without a clue as to the culprit. If Loran could offer any help at all, it would be better than what they had to this point.

Loran's smirk faded and he regarded first Raedrick and then Julian with unblinking, probing eyes for a relative eternity.

Finally, he let out his breath in an annoyed sigh and nodded, very slightly. "Very well."

He leaned his staff back against the wall and settled down into the chair he had just vacated. Leaning back in the chair, he teepled his fingers together in front of his chest and fixed the two of them with a look so severe, so commanding, that Julian found himself unable to look away.

"I am here on Magestirium business."

Not this again. "You said that before - " Julian's jaw snapped shut, cutting off his words as Loran's gaze became something deathly hard.

"I did. And you would have been wise to pay heed to my words. Were it not for your meddling, I may have brought the recent misfortune to an end days ago."

Julian squirmed on his feet, trying in vain to look away.

Loran remained silent for a time, his scowl returning in spades as he watched Julian. Then, finally, he shook his head. "I suppose you cannot be blamed for your ignorance. I sometimes forget how little the uninitiated understand of the real world." That evoked a slight grin from the Mage. Somehow that was even more disconcerting than the scowl.

Loran broke the stare with Julian and put his attention fully back onto Raedrick. "I came here in pursuit of a fugitive, one I have been tracking for some time. He passed through Mangin City a few weeks ago. There were only a very few places he could have gone from there, and I had tracers set up in all of them." His eyebrow quirked upward again. "Except here."

"And you did not inform us." Raedrick's words came out coldly, laced with entire layers of accusation.

"Of course not. He is a member of the Magestirium, not some chattel subject to your laws. And anyway, you could not wield power over such as he even if you had the right to make the attempt."

Raedrick had no response to that, apparently. He just scowled. He did not like the fact that Loran was right about the limits of their jurisdiction any more than Julian did. Far less actually, Julian was willing to bet.

"What did he do?" Julian asked. It had to be something big.

Loran's lips twisted into an expression of distaste. "You are familiar with the theorem of parallel universes."

Julian blinked his eyes. The what of the what? Raedrick looked as clueless as Julian felt.

The expression of distaste on Loran's face became one of disgust. He rolled his eyes. "The alternate planes of existence?"

Oh. That. "Why didn't you say so?"

Julian only thought Loran looked disgusted before. The look the Mage shot him was... Well, Julian had seen his General look at a new recruit who had just been convicted of cowardice before the enemy once. The General had more respect in his eyes than Loran did just then.

The Mage inhaled deeply and closed his eyes for a moment as though trying to will himself to calm. Then, very slowly, he said, "There are beings who live on other planes of existence than the world we know. Some of them are the entities we call the Gods, though that is far from an accurate description and gives most of them more credit than they are due."

"Don't let the temple priests here you say that," Raedrick said wryly.

Loran shrugged. "The ignorant always apply supernatural properties or divinity to the things they do not understand." He sniffed and made a dismissive gesture. "They count for nothing. The important thing is that these beings exist, and with skill and care, can be contacted. Some are benign. Others..." He trailed off and lifted an eyebrow meaningfully.

Julian swallowed. He had a bad feeling he knew where this was going.

"The fugitive made a practice of communicating with the Out-dwellers, as we call them. This is not unusual amongst the more skilled of our order. But he..." Loran shook his head. "He became obsessed. At some point, he began to believe he had a special bond with one being in particular, that he was this being's ambassador to the material world. Or maybe his Avatar. It is difficult to know the ravings of a broken mind. Regardless, he resisted all attempts to dissuade him from his studies until finally, we were forced to bar him from entrance to the facilities where trans-planar contact can be performed."

"I imagine he did not react well to that."

Loran nodded at Raedrick's words. "Though we did not know how poorly for some time. He disappeared into relative obscurity, and we presumed that, unable to continue that path, he found other avenues of study to occupy himself." He sighed. "That presumption ended up being...unwise. Corpses began appearing in the city. Thieves, whores, drunks. A few here and there, horribly mutilated. But at first no one paid them much mind, because who really cares if the dregs of society turn up dead? Better for all concerned, no?"

"No." Raedrick's voice was hard.

Loran's eyebrow quirked upward, but his expression remained smooth. "But then a member of the Magestirium turned up dead, in his quarters. I do not need to describe how his body was arranged; you have seen it. His name was Mattios, and he led the commission that sat in judgment on our fugitive. An investigation revealed a startling truth: he had been killed by non-human magical means."

"Non-human?" Julian said. "That doesn't..."

"Make any sense?" Loran made a soft tsking sound. "We thought the same. It was only after two more of our brothers turned up dead that we realized the truth. The fugitive had somehow designed a way to bring his familiar Out-dweller into our world. He set the Out-dweller against those he considered immoral, and it was happy to oblige, to sate its hunger for pain and terror. Then, once he was sure of their alliance, he turned the

Out-dweller on the members of our order he believed had betrayed him.

"We attempted to take him into custody, but he managed to evade us. Four of our inquisitors were killed in the process. He fled into the country, and we've been looking for him ever since. He left signs of his passage: corpses, mostly. Always mutilated in the same way, always people on the fringe of society or morally corrupt in some way. It has been speculated that he targets them out of some deluded notion that he is doing good, but more likely the Out-dweller prefers the taste of such dregs."

Julian rocked back on his heels, stunned by the mage's account. He had never heard of anything that even came close to matching this. Ever. He glanced at Raedrick and saw that his friend was similarly taken aback, though he hid it well behind an implacable mask.

"Does this fugitive have a name?" Raedrick asked.

"Of course. But I will not speak it. He knows he is being hunted, and it is perfectly within his capability to enact tracer spells that will let him know when his name is spoken, where, and by whom."

"So?" Julian said incredulously. "He has to know you're in town, if he's here. You've not exactly been keeping out of sight."

"There is a good chance he may not. He tends to keep out of public places, preferring hidey-holes and the like. But even if he has seen me, he cannot know I am hunting him specifically."

That was a big assumption. Not one Julian would have been comfortable making, were he in Loran's shoes. But whatever; what the mage did with his skin was his own business.

"If this man is as dangerous as you say," Raedrick said, "dangerous enough to kill four of your order during his escape, how is it you are here alone?"

Julian nodded. "Yeah, I would want backup if I were you."

"Then it is a very good thing you are not me, Constable," Loran replied. He leaned back in his chair and regarded the pair of them for a moment, then smirked. "I am quite capable of dealing with him. He was my student, before he went awry. He was never my equal, and that remains true to this day."

Hubris, thy name is Loran. But again, it was his skin to risk. Just so long as he stayed away from -

"Alright. So how can we help?"

Julian looked incredulously at Raedrick. Was he nuts? Defending the townsfolk was one thing, but they had neither the expertise nor the equipment to deal with this rogue mage and his pet whatever-Loran-called-it. Better to let Loran handle it, if he was so certain he could. Julian opened his mouth to say that very thing, but he was silenced by the determined look in Raedrick's eyes.

Julian suppressed an inward groan. There would be no getting through to him; when Raedrick had that expression he was as stubborn as a mule.

Loran snorted. "Just stay out of my way."

Raedrick quirked an eyebrow at the mage. "You were here for quite a while before we," he flashed an apologetic smile, "picked you up, but you were not able to find him. Seems to me having local assistance can only be helpful."

The mage shook his head. "He is using concealing magic, but there are ways to see past that sort of thing, or to track the magical residue left by its use. His trail was fresh. I would have found him rather quickly, except..." He stopped talking, frowning as though unsure whether to proceed or not.

"Except what?" Julian said. He did not get to play the mysterious mage anymore, not now.

Loran looked at him and for a second Julian thought the mage was going to rip his head off. But then, instead, Loran sighed and nodded as though coming to a decision. "Except he has found an ally here."

Julian's jaw dropped open and he felt like he had been hit by a tone of bricks.

"What?" Raedrick sounded more angry than shocked.

"He has an ally. At least one. At first I was only able to detect one person's concealment spell. But then, about a day after I arrived, a second individual began using concealing magic here."

"Wait. You can tell when different people cast different spells?"

Loran smirked. "Of course. Every practitioner is different, has his own unique temperament and focus when he casts a spell. That uniqueness passes on into his spells, and if one is knowledgable and skilled enough, one can pick out those unique elements."

"I had no idea," Raedrick said, turning eyes that were suddenly troubled toward Julian for a heartbeat before looking back at Loran and carefully schooling his face back to calm.

Julian swallowed, suddenly feeling faint with tension as his heart leapt into his throat. That second residue could only come from one person.

"It is not an easy talent to master," Loran said, looking amused at their reactions, "but it is quite useful. There is something familiar about the accomplice's residue. I can't quite put my finger on it, but..." He shrugged. "No matter. I will located them both, and they will answer for their crimes, not just against the Magestirium but against your people as well, I assure you. It is only a matter of time."

Loran smiled at them confidently and his dark eyes twinkled with cold anticipation. Just then, he looked like a predator getting ready to leap upon an unwary prey.

THE GUILTY PARTY

"Melanie! Open up!"

Julian pounded on the door to Melanie's shop, heedless of the CLOSED sign hanging in the window. He had to find her before... He put that thought out of his mind. He did not want to consider what would happen if—no, when—Loran caught up to her. She had convinced herself that he was not looking for her, and he was not. But now she had unwittingly placed herself in his sights. The situation was precarious, and she did not even know it.

Of course there was no answer. She had not opened her store in days. Julian would not have put it past her to have stayed beneath one of her concealments spells more or less continuously since they let her know of Loran's presence in town. A great idea, but now it was one that would get her caught.

Julian backed away from the door and had to hold back a snarl borne of frustration and worry. He peered up to the shop's second story, where Melanie made her residence. The windows were dark, the curtains drawn. There was no indication she was upstairs at all, and surely she would have come down when she heard his knock. Where could she be?

"Dammit," he muttered.

This was taking too long. He glanced up at the sun; just past noon. He was due to meet back up with Raedrick soon. He had gone to fill the Mayor in on the developments with Loran. Ordinarily Julian would have gone with him, but Melanie needed to be warned. Raedrick had not objected to Julian taking the task of finding her, and the Gods knew Julian was more than happy to avoid that meeting with the Mayor. So he bowed out. It almost made him feel a tiny bit guilty.

Almost.

The lack of Melanie was a problem, though. Julian considered leaving a note, but shelved that idea as being too risky. And besides, he did not have any paper with him. So, with a sigh, he turned away from Melanie's shop. She would just have to take care of herself, for the time being at least.

Raedrick was just emerging from City Hall when Julian got there. He looked his normal self: well-tailored clothes and boots that, despite being common in cut, still somehow managed to give him a swashbuckling look. His expression was calm. Only a tightness about his eyes revealed how wound up he was.

"That bad?"

Raedrick shrugged, but winced slightly before he was able to school his face to smoothness. "About as expected."

Julian nodded. "That bad."

Raedrick coughed out a half-chuckle and flashed a grin that almost made it to his eyes. "Any luck?"

Julian shook his head.

"Damn." He drew in a breath and held it for a few seconds before exhaling slowly and smoothly. It was a calming exercise that Raedrick had picked up somewhere. He tried to teach it to the squad, back in the Army, but as far as Julian was concerned it never seemed to work any better than anything else. It looked like it worked ok for Raedrick today, at least. "Well, we'll just have to keep an eye out for her and hope she doesn't cross paths with Loran. In the meantime, though, we have an appointment."

Julian quirked a questioning eyebrow at him.

Raedrick saw the expression. "Remember what Loran said? His fugitive and his pet Out-dweller only killed people who were morally compromised."

Julian nodded.

"How do you supposed this fellow decided that Baelin and Beverlee fit the bill? I never heard a whisper that there was anything going on between them. Did you?"

That was for certain. It had been a bit of a shock learning of their affair, and not just because Beverlee never seemed interested in any man. Baelin was not exactly well-known in town, as much time as he spent off in the woods, but everyone regarded him as a fine family man who put his wife and children first above all things.

Well, apparently not above all things, after all.

Julian shook his head, his brain making the logical leap before Raedrick could voice it for him. "Only Isla and Helena knew, and of the two of them..."

"Only Ilsa had reason to wish them ill," Raedrick finished.

So they were back to Ilsa being the culprit once again. Just in a different manner than they initially thought.

This was going to be one hell of an interesting appointment.

Ilsa answered the door herself when Julian knocked.

She looked horrid. Her eyes were sunken, with dark circles beneath them that scream she had not been sleeping. Little strands of hair stood up in wisps atop her head, having pulled free from the bun she wore. How long had it been since she last did her hair up? For that matter, her dress was rumpled. Had she slept—or rather not slept—in it?

Ilsa's eyes flicked between him and Raedrick and Julian saw

fright competing with resignation for a moment. "I said before I've got nothing else to say to you."

"We know who killed Baelin, Ilsa," Raedrick said. "And Beverlee."

She blinked and fell back a half-step, letting the door swing open an additional foot before she caught herself. "What?" Her voice quavered a bit. From her expression, she had to work hard to keep it from doing more. "Who?"

"Did anyone else other than you know about Baelin and Beverlee's affair?" Julian said.

Ilsa swallowed and opened her mouth as if to speak, but no words came out. After several seconds, she sighed and lowered his eyes. Then she stepped back and let the door swing open fully.

"You'd better come inside." Her voice as she spoke was defeated, seemingly devoid of hope. She did not wait for them to respond, but turned her back and walked further into her house, She quickly disappeared around a corner.

Julian exchanged a quick glance with Raedrick, then followed her in.

They found her in a small sitting room at the end of the cottage, adjacent to the home's small cooking area. It was sparsely appointed, but what furniture there was was well-crafted, by Baelin's own hand Julian wagered. Several small drawings were stuck on the walls, the children's handiwork from the look of them, and a faint, pleasant aroma permeated the room. It was from some manner of spices that Julian could not put his finger on, but the scent leant the final touch to make the room feel warm and welcoming.

Or at least it would have under different circumstances.

Isla sat in a rocking chair in the far corner of the room, gazing at the floor and wearing the most pained expression Julian had seen on her during this whole episode. She had not looked that mournful at Baelin's funeral.

"Where are the children?" Raedrick asked as he came to a halt in the center of the room.

"School," Ilsa said in a monotone

Julian blinked in surprise. As far as he knew, Ilsa did all the schooling for her children herself. "Come again?"

She snorted out a half-laugh. "Helena came by yesterday. Said she felt horrible for everything that had happened. 'Bout time she felt bad." Her lips twisted into a snarl for a moment, but then just as quickly fell back into their earlier defeated frown. It was like Ilsa's face did not have the energy to support her being angry. She continued in that same monotone. "I was about to kick her off my land when she offered to teach them free of charge." Another snorted laugh. "Can you believe it?"

Raedrick sounded incredulous as he said, "And you accepted?"

Ilsa shrugged. "I wanted to tell her to shove her teaching up..." She stopped speaking, flushing a bit for a moment before she cleared her throat and continued. "But I thought about what it could mean to them to get properly schooled." Another shrug. "I don't care if it makes the hussy feel better about things, but if it does my children some good... I can pretend."

Julian cleared his throat. "You told Melanie Klemins that you had a serious problem you needed to discuss, but you never told her what. You meant Baelin and Beverlee, didn't you?"

Ilsa merely nodded.

He exchanged another look with Raedrick. His friend looked resolved, but also pained, as though dreading to hear this. Julian could relate.

Julian waited for a moment, hoping Raedrick would pick up the line of questioning. And so silence loomed for a long moment.

"I couldn't go to her," Ilsa said before Julian could give voice to the next question. "It'd be all over town, and then..." Her voice broke and for a second or two it looked as though she was going to dissolve into a fit of weeping. But then she surprised Julian. She straightened her back and raised her eyes from the floor for the first time since they walked in. "If she could not help, no one could, so I decided to drink instead."

"Uh..." Julian began.

Ilsa quirked an eyebrow at him. "I went to Holb's, and was having a merry time of it. Until *he* showed up." Her expression darkened, then reverted back to its earlier hopeless and defeated mask, and she lowered her eyes once again.

"He?" Julian said, and was surprised at how hesitant, how uncertain, he sounded.

Ilsa nodded. "The one you're looking for."

Raedrick perked up, his entire body seeming to spring forward in a rush even though all he did was take a half-step toward the woman, and a slow half-step at that. "Who is he?"

Ilsa shrugged. "Never got his name. Never saw him before that night, either. I was sitting at the end of the bar, and he sat down on a stool next to me. I remember thinking it had been a long time since a nice looking man had tried to approach me socially, and he had this look in his eye..." She shivered visibly. "It made me remember."

"Ah," Julian began, "That's..."

Ilsa cut him off. Though in reality she did not seem to have heard him, or at least she did not seem to care that he was speaking. She just kept right on talking as though he did not exist. "He said he could see that my heart was troubled, that I had been done wrong." She drew a quick breath and held it. When she finally exhaled, it was like a sigh of regret, tinged with longing. "He said a woman as lovely as I am should never be heartsick like I was." Tears welled up in Ilsa's eyes and began to run down her cheeks. "How could he have known how I was feeling so clearly? How desolate my heart was?" She sobbed softly and pressed her hand to her mouth in a vain attempt to hold her emotion back.

Julian looked away, embarrassed for her despite their suspicions about her culpability in her husband's death. A man did not intrude on a lady's grief unless invited, after all. From the corner of his eye, he saw Raedrick doing the same.

After a pause that seemed to take forever, Ilsa sniffed and wiped the tears away. Then her voice gained a little bit of strength. "I told the man about my suspicions about Baelin and

Beverlee. I knew Baelin had a little hideaway in the woods some-where. I didn't know where, but I was certain they met there for their little trysts."

Raedrick's voice was quiet, but hard as steel. "And what did this man do?"

"Nothing. At least nothing right then. He patted my hand, bought me a drink, and said that if my husband had truly betrayed me in that way, he would get what was coming to him." She shuddered. "When he touched me, it was like nothing I had ever felt before. It sent a shiver up my arm and to my brain. But it was a good shiver. It made me feel like everything was going to be alright, that he would make all my troubles go away."

"What happened then?" Julian asked.

Ilsa did not move her head, but her eyes lifted to look at them. "I do not remember anything after that except waking in my bedroom here. Alone." She shivered again and wrapped her arms around herself as though to ward off the winter's chill. "Later the next day, you found Baelin dead."

It was not entirely unexpected, but the flat way she said it made Julian's blood run cold. "You think this man killed him." It was not a question.

Ilsa hesitated, then nodded.

"Why did you not come to us before?"

She sniffed back another round of tears. Or at least it looked like another round was due any moment, anyway. "What would I have told you? That I met some strange man in a bar and he whis-pered in my ear all night, and I couldn't remember anything after that? What would you have thought of me?"

Julian opened his mouth to retort, then shut it as the reality of her words sank in. What *would* he have thought? That she was running around on her husband and had remorse after the fact, that's what. Slowly, reluctantly, he nodded, acknowledging her point.

"It was not until Beverlee was killed also that I began to suspect. And by then..." She broke off and turned her head away again, raising a clenched fist to her mouth as she fought to hold back another sob.

She did not need to say it. By then, if she had come forward then, with a story as full of holes as this, she would have been high on the list of suspects, if not the only one.

Then again, she was high on the suspect list anyway, so a lot of good her silence did for her.

"What did this man look like?" Raedrick asked, softly, in the tone he reserved for the most delicate situations.

Ilsa shook her head. "I can't remember. The only thing I can remember is his voice. It was so soft." She drew a shuddering breath. "So soft..."

Raedrick and Julian exchanged glances. She was acting like a woman who was not entirely in her right mind. But then, Julian supposed that made sense, if the man she encountered was the fugitive Loran described. Who knew what a mage who was demented enough to kill - or have his other-worldly minion kill - in the way he had would, or could, do to an unwitting victim's mind?

Raedrick, as usual, had an easier time keeping his investigative wits about it. "Do you think you could recognize his voice if you heard it again?"

Ilsa nodded emphatically, but said not a word.

Raedrick returned the nod. "Thank you, Ilsa." He turned to leave.

Julian was about to turn to go when a thought struck him. "Where was Baelin's hideaway?" He almost smiled when he saw Raedrick stop abruptly, stiffening as he realized what he had missed.

Ilsa did not look at them. She just shrugged. "I don't know. Somewhere in the woods, above a big stone cliff." Her voice returned to its earlier, haunted monotone. "That's all he ever said about it."

Julian looked at her, and despite everything felt his heart going out for her. She had lost everything, and yes she may have borne some of the blame for what happened, but only a little. How could she have known who - what - she was talking to? He saw clearly the grief in her eyes, almost buried beneath mountains of confusion and guilt, and he knew there was nothing he could say to make it better.

But there might be something he could *do*.

He turned and brushed past Raedrick on his way out of the cottage. That renegade mage was going to *pay*.

❧ 20 ❧

SUSPECT

"**J**ulian," Raedrick said, his tone concerned but also stern in that way that he got when he was talking with a subordinate who had done something stupid. He should know better than that. He was not Julian's superior officer, not any more. They were friends, partners. Equals.

"I've had about enough of this," Julian growled, not slowing his pace. In fact, he sped up. He glanced up at the sun and did a quick computation in his head. About an hour after noon. Holb ought to be getting ready to open up.

"So have I," Raedrick said. "But what do you think you're going to accomplish running off in a fury like this?"

"Watch me."

Raedrick tried several times to speak with him over the intervening minutes that it took to reach Holb's Tavern, but he would have none of it. Their killer had been there, just a few nights ago. He had seduced Ilsa - maybe seduced was not the correct term, but how else to think about one person warping another's thoughts and perceptions to his will? - and someone must surely have taken note of him.

Holb was just rolling up the canvas tarp that blocked the bar off from the elements when Julian arrived, Raedrick on his heels.

Funny how he had gotten quiet as soon as he saw their destination.

The large tavern-keeper eyed Julian with something between curiosity and annoyance as he approached, then he grunted. The grunt spoke volumes. What the hell did *he* want?

"The night before Baelin the woodsman died, a man approached his wife here, at your bar."

Holb grunted again, then turned back to the tarp and began tying it in place.

Julian ground his teeth. "I am certain that man is the one responsible for the murders."

Holb froze in place, his fingers in the middle of a knot that Julian had no doubt he would never be able to tie himself. Holb turned his head slightly and looked at them, his face implacable but one eyebrow twitching upward.

"Did you see him?"

Holb did not make a sound for several seconds. Then he rolled his eyes slightly and turned back to the knot. He finished it off with a swift tug of his wrists and turned around, wiping his hands on the apron he always wore behind the bar. For a moment, Julian wondered at the inanity of wearing that apron now, so far before his normal opening time. But only for a moment.

Holb cleared his throat and shrugged. "Saw a guy talking wit 'er," he said, his deep gravelly voice sounding thoroughly unconcerned. The glimmer of anger, and fear, in his eyes put the lie to his indifference. "Medium height, medium build. Light brown hair, tanned skin, like Selam." He frowned thoughtfully. "Aside from that, just looked sort of...average." He shrugged and turned back to the middle of the bar, where the next tie that held the tarp up dangled, ready to be fastened in place.

Raedrick finally broke his silence. "An average person. That's it. That's all you have."

Holb glanced back at him over his shoulder, and his frown turned into something that was more like a scowl. He held

Raedrick's gaze for a second, then shook his head again and got back to tying the next knot.

"Have you seen him before, or since?"

Holb paused again, pondering, then shrugged as he pulled the knot tight. "Only saw him one other time. He was talkin' wit Dewey the other night."

"The same night Dewey was killed." It was not a question.

Holb froze still, then jerked out a nod. If Julian did not know him better, he would have sworn the big barkeep was spooked.

Julian looked over at Raedrick and saw his friend chewing on his lower lip, lost in thought. The wheels were turning quickly behind Raedrick's eyes, but Julian was fairly certain he knew where Raedrick was going. No one is average. No one. There is always *some* distinguishing characteristic about a person. Most people may not notice those characteristics, but they are there, and Julian was fairly certain Holb was not the type to miss those sorts of things. If *he* could only describe the guy as average, there was something else at work.

Magic.

There could be no doubt about it. They had finally found the trail of their killer. For a second Julian felt a surge of elation run up his spine. It quickly faded before reality. Sure they knew where the killer had been, and more or less what he was, assuming Loran had been truthful with his tale. But they still had no idea where the hell to even start looking for his lair.

Raedrick spoke up. "One more thing, Holb."

The bartender sent an icy gaze Raedrick's way and, if anything, scowled even more deeply.

Raedrick seemed not to notice. "Did Baelin ever come in here?"

Holb shrugged and gave a half-nod. The woodsman did not come by often, the nod said, but every now and then.

"Did you ever hear him talk about his hideaway in the woods? Where it was?"

Holb rolled his eyes slightly, then gave a quick shake of his head and turned away completely. It was obvious from the set of his shoulders that he did not intend to say another word to them.

Well, that had been better than nothing. *Far* better.

Raedrick looked more than a trifle reluctant as he raised his hand to knock on Loran's door, and Julian did not blame him. The mage had re-claimed his room at The Oarlock, but if Molli's extremely terse warning was any indication, he was in no mood for visitors.

Small wonder, that.

All in all, Julian considered that maybe going to him was not the best idea he had ever had. Hell, Raedrick as much as pointed that out, even though he was in agreement. They had uncovered an important lead, and Loran needed to learn about it, both because it might help him to finish his work and get out of town as soon as possible and because it would show they had some value to contribute. Ordinarily, Julian could not have cared less about what someone like him thought, but if he and Raedrick could convince Loran to let them on the team, they could work more efficiently towards capturing the rogue bastard.

And, maybe, keep Loran away from Melanie.

The door opened, and the mage looked out at the two of them with a quirked eyebrow. He was dressed in his formal robes, the same as he had worn to meet the Mayor, which seemed a bit odd.

"Constables. Have you come to escort me to the funeral?"

Julian blinked and traded a surprised look with Raedrick. "Ah...beg pardon?" he said.

Loran's eyebrow quirked up even higher. "The funeral for Master Dewey and that unfortunate young woman is this evening, is it not?"

Julian nodded, confused. As with Beverlee, the decision had been made to not delay any more than necessary. But Loran had not come to any of the funerals so far. Why would he care to come to this one?

Loran sniffed softly, dismissively. "If you're not to be my escorts, I would ask you to leave me in peace. I have preparations to make before I depart for the ceremony."

He began to push the door closed, but Raedrick pressed his palm against it, stopping its motion. "We need to talk."

"I think not. Last we talked, you were none too cordial or cooperative. As I said, leave me be. And maybe I will forget your transgressions when I make my report to the Magestirium." Loran smiled a nasty little smile that said his earlier forgiveness was not on the up and up. Not that Julian really expected it to be. "Or at least, I could lessen their severity."

Raedrick just gave him a level look. "We have information about the killer's identity."

Loran's smile slipped and he regarded first Raedrick and then Julian with a frank, appraising stare. Then, after a long moment he sighed softly and pulled the door fully open, waving for them to enter his room.

Loran frowned deeply when Raedrick finished telling what they had learned from Ilsa and Holb. He sat on the lone chair in the room, looking up at the two of them like a ruler receiving supplicants. Julian had to work hard to avoid letting his irritation with the man's demeanor show.

But then, he had to remind himself that they had put Loran out considerably over the last couple of days. A little smugness in payback was taking it rather light, to be honest.

Loran teepled his fingers in the air beneath his chin and did not speak for a good minute. When he finally replied, he spoke slowly, like a man tasting his thoughts before he let them pass his lips. Like a man reading a judge's sentence. "Thank you, Constables. This is most helpful."

Julian thought sure he was going to say something more, but after a couple seconds passed, he shrugged lamely.

Loran saw the gesture and smirked ever so slightly. "I mean it sincerely, Constable Hinderbrook. This information provides a great insight into the fugitive's next action."

"Ah... It does?"

"Indeed."

Silence loomed for another long several seconds. Loran looked at them expectantly the whole while. Finally, when it seemed the awkwardness of the moment could grow no larger, he rolled his eyes and spoke again. "Thank you gentlemen. That will be all."

"Magester Haversted," Raedrick said, "I really think..."

"I am well aware of what you are thinking, Constable." Loran tapped his right index finger against his temple, and Julian's blood ran cold. Gods above, he really could read their minds!

Raedrick snorted loudly. "Don't try that old trick. We're not a couple of bumpkins whose knowledge of the world goes no further than the edge of our village."

Julian glanced at his friend and swallowed. He was glad Raedrick, at least, was sure that particular rumor was untrue. For his part, Julian had never heard anything definitive either way - and hang it all, why had he never asked Melanie about it? But then, maybe as Squad Leader Raedrick received more detailed briefings, or met some of the Division's mages, or some such.

Loran looked at Raedrick for a couple seconds, then he smiled, a far more genuine smile than he had shown to either of them to date. He let out a soft chuckle and raised a hand in a mollifying gesture. "Say your peace, Constable."

Raedrick gave a quick nod, then continued. "We know he's been to Holb's twice, and that he picked his victims because of what he learned from Ilsa. We have information on where Baelin's hideaway is. I'll bet good money he went there a time or two, since Beverlee and Baelin met there. If..."

"Yes, yes," Loran said, waving dismissively. "I've seen this hideaway. A thoroughly unimpressive little shack. Unimportant."

Raedrick blinked. "What?"

"I'll tell you what *is* important, Constable." He leaned forward, peering intently at Raedrick. "You know why Baelin and Beverlee were killed: the affair. The young woman at the boarding house was almost certainly a case of being in the wrong place at the wrong time." He inhaled slowly, then spread his hands and asked, "But why was Dewey the woodsman killed as well?"

Raedrick opened his mouth to reply but paused. He looked perplexed after a second or so and closed his mouth again.

The question caught Julian off guard as well. If Loran's fugitive went after the morally depraved, Beverlee and Baelin were prime targets, because of their adultery. Dewey though... Julian did not know enough about Dewey to be able to say one way or the other what sort of man he really was. He had no idea about Dewey's habits except for the little he had observed during their tromp into the Glamorwood together, but Dewey did not have a bad reputation. So why would he...

It hit him all at once. He could not believe they had not seen it before. "Dewey knew about the affair and did not stop it," Julian said.

Loran turned his eyes on Julian and nodded, his expression almost approving. "Now. Did anyone else know this thing was going on?"

Julian's blood ran cold again. Frigid. "Helena." He had to forced the name out from between his lips.

"The dead harridan's sister, yes. She also did nothing to stop the affair," Loran said, "and so is equally guilty." He raised a forestalling hand as Raedrick opened his mouth to retort. "Or at least that argument could be made by someone who is less interested in truth than on wreaking vengeance. Someone like the fugitive to his Out-Dweller consort."

Raedrick's expression was beyond troubled. "You expect him to make a try for Helena. When?"

Loran shrugged. "If it were me, I would wait until after the funeral. More dramatic that way, more symbolic. He'll wait until later tonight, then he'll hunt her down and..." He left the rest unsaid.

"Bugger me," Julian breathed. "Well, at least we know where he's going to strike next."

Loran looked between Raedrick and Julian for another long couple of seconds, then sighed and shook his head. "I see that it is useless to tell you to remain clear of this." He stood up and smoothed out his robes. "Very well. Since you insist of butting in, you may assist."

"Assist with what?" Julian said, though he had a feeling he already knew the answer.

Sure enough, Loran grinned, a hunter's grin that showed his teeth. His canines seemed to gleam in the afternoon sunlight that streamed in through his window. "We are going to set a trap for this killer, this very night."

21

PREDATOR AND PREY

J ulian shivered and pulled his cloak more tightly against his body. It was a chilly night, and dark with only a faint sliver of moon in the sky, and the mail he had donned earlier certainly did not help matters. But it was not solely the temperature that made Julian shiver. This was dangerous business they were on, and he was not entirely certain they were ready for it.

Oh sure, Loran put on a good show of confidence, circling around Beverlee and Helena's house with his staff dragging on the ground while he chanted in a low tone and in words - if they even *were* words - from no language Julian ever heard before. He was certainly casting a spell of some sort, but Julian only knew enough about magecraft to be able to tell when a man is casting a spell. He had no idea as to what that spell may do.

Julian glanced up at the stairs leading up the side of the house toward Helena and Beverlee's flat. Helena had moved back in just yesterday. Far sooner than he would have expected, but the men the town hired to clean up the mess had been thorough and she could not have much money stashed away to cover her rent and a room at an Inn or boarding house.

Strange that she did not have some friends who would let her stay with them, but she and Beverlee had kept to themselves, except with the children. And, apparently, with other women's husbands.

It almost made Julian wonder what Helena did in her private time. Like sister, like sister, perhaps?

He pushed that thought away. Even if it were true, it had no bearing on the night's mission: to save her life. Assuming Loran was correct, that was.

Just then, the mage finished his incantations and stopped, leaning on his staff for a good half minute. Julian blinked to see him breathing heavily, as after a hard bit of effort. But all he had done was walk a circle and chant. Strange, that.

Loran straightened and turned toward where Julian and Raedrick stood, at the front corner of the sisters' building. He favored them with the briefest of nods, then said, "It is done."

"What, exactly?" Raedrick voiced Julian's words just as plainly as he would have.

"A warding of sorts. It will alert me when the Out-Dweller crosses within, and take certain steps to reduce its power while it remains. Even the two of you could take it, if it came down to it, as long as it remained within the warding."

Julian whistled softly, the mage's barb ignored in the face of his explanation. From what the mage had said, this Out-Dweller thing was no slouch. If the warding was as good as he claimed, it was no wonder it had tired him out, casting it.

Loran smirked and glanced at Julian. "Best you not test that theory, though. I will take it. *Your* job," he added in a pointed, commanding tone, "is to ensure no surprises creep up on me while I do it. Understand?"

Julian glowered, but Raedrick nodded immediately so he followed suit. No sense griping, he supposed, but it still irked him, how Loran talked down at them sometimes. Most times.

The mage smirked again, then turned and walked up the stairs to the door leading into the sisters' flat. There, he retreated in the shadows of the entrance and effectively vanished from sight.

"I hope this works," Julian said, his gaze lingering on where Loran waited. "I don't like the notion of using Helena as bait."

"Me neither." Raedrick's frown spoke volumes that his tone did not. "But he's probably right. If she *is* the target they - it - will follow her wherever she is."

Julian nodded reluctantly. "I still don't like it."

Raedrick clapped him on the shoulder and they shared a grim smile before retreating to their positions. Julian settled into the deeper shadows beneath the eaves of the house to the sisters' left, Raedrick to a small alcove in the building to the right.

And then they settled down to wait.

Melanie stood in the doorway of a butcher's shop across the way from Beverlee and Helena's building, behind the veil of her concealment spell, and watched Loran complete his circle of enchantment. She frowned, recognizing parts of the incantation, or at least the movements Loran used, enough to figure out that he was setting up a warding of some sort, but she had never seen one quite like what he just made.

She only managed to catch fractions of the conversation between the three men as she followed them from The Oarlock, where she had been waiting for Loran to make an appearance, but she did not like the sound of the situation at all. "Out-Dweller" was not a title to make anyone learned about such things feel comfortable.

Truth be told, she had to force herself to keep her feet in place, lest she flee to a place of safety. If only half the things Timon told her about them were true, Julian and Raedrick were in far more danger than they knew.

And Loran as well.

She sniffed softly, ignoring that part of her mind. She did not care one whit if Loran put himself in danger or not. If he were butchered alive or not. He had...

Memories, pushed aside for so long, flooded back. Timon's smile, kind and warm. The feel of his arms around her. The joy, the *wonder*, of their time together. The heart-wrenching sound of his agonized screams when they took him. And the decision to flee, to save herself, that left her heart broken and bleeding on the stones behind her as she went, never to be whole again.

They had spoken of it. Of the danger they both faced from his teaching her, and he had made her promise to do just that, if they were discovered: to run. But that did not make it any easier, or lessen her guilt over abandoning him.

Melanie shuddered and drew in a deep breath to get herself under control. She swiped at the little tears that had fallen partway down her cheeks, her returned grief changing to anger, a towering fury. She would not wallow in her tears again. Especially not now, not when she had the opportunity to strike at the source of all her pain.

She reached into the pouch that hung from her belt opposite her dagger and fingered through its contents. She knew each by touch, components that would help bring her spells to life. Oh, the things she could do, the pain she could weave onto the Inquisitor's form before he perished!

The men exchanged a few words, then Loran retreated up the stairs and Julian and Raedrick took up their positions. Their trap, and it surely could be nothing else, was set.

Just as she had hoped.

A battle with an Out-Dweller would be taxing, even with the warding, whatever it did. Loran would be exhausted once it was done. And then she...

A subtle sound, so low in pitch that it almost did not register with her ears, interrupted Melanie's train of thought.

She looked around, frowning, unable to tell the sound's source.

A shiver went up her spine, and she found herself trembling. There was something about that noise. Something...unclean. Ominous.

The sound increased in volume and she began to make out a rhythm to it. A steady beat that made her heart race as it grew louder. It took a full minute for her to recognize the sound for that it was: footsteps.

Melanie panned around, seeking the source of the footsteps, but it was in vain. All was darkness and shadow except for the suddenly very tiny-seeming nimbuses of light around the street lamps scattered at irregular intervals. This section of Lydelton was not as well-lit as Main Street by any means, and even there the Lamplighters were sparing with their services.

Nothing moved, and yet something did. It crept - no, not crept, stalked - closer. Melanie could feel its presence, a palpable weight in her mind, and felt the first stirrings of panic. This was the thing nightmares were made of.

Fitting that it comes now, in the dead of night. For it is death on the hunt. Come for you.

Where had that thought come from? Melanie shook her head to clear it, but the mental weight only got worse.

She smelled it. Faint on the night breeze at first, but growing steadily stronger as the thing advanced. Sickly-sweet, like fruit that had been left out too long and went rancid. It left her twisting uncomfortably, as if all the other stimuli were not enough.

Again she looked about. Still nothing, but it could not be long now. She glanced back at the shadowy areas where her friends - and her nemesis - waited. They must be feeling the Out-Dweller's approach, as she did. In her mind's eye, she saw Julian and Raedrick draw their weapons, bolstering their courage against this sudden terror with the reassuring feel of cold steel, useless though that steel would be against this foe.

The slightest shifting of a shadow off to the left drew her eyes, and for a second all Melanie could see was darkness. Then the darkness itself seemed to move, to slither through the intervening space between one building and the next, and the hairs on Melanie's neck stood up straight. Even beneath the crushing pressure she felt in her mind, she knew.

It had come. The Out-Dweller.

May the Gods help them.

❧ 22 ❧

THE OUT-DWELLER

The Out-Dweller moved quickly, more quickly than the pace of its footsteps would have suggested. In the darkness, Melanie almost could not follow its progress toward the sisters' building. She realized she was more than trembling; she was shaking from head to toe, the Out-Dweller's presence had affected her so. Part of her mind recoiled at her reaction, shouting defiance at the fear and demanding she get ahold of herself and Do. Something.

The more sensible part of herself replied that the best thing to do was keep back, out of sight, and pray the beast did not notice her.

It did not seem to. It kept to its course, a darker shadow that made the other shadows recoil in terror as it sped toward its target.

And then it stopped cold, and for an instant Melanie beheld it, in all its perversion.

Shadows wrapped the creature from head to toe, standing out against the backdrop of a lonely street lamp like a bird before the sun. Darkness swirled and swayed, obscuring the being beneath so that only portions could be seen in any particular instant. Short legs that ended in cloven hooves. A mammoth, hulking torso that was covered in spikes and barbs. Long arms that reached past its knees and ended in long, curved talons. A small round head. Or was it large, capped by horns? Or twin heads, laughing insanely at the world around them? The cloak of darkness made it difficult to see anything for certain there except for two pairs of eyes that glowed red like the depths of a smith's forge.

A new sound reached Melanie's ears. Higher pitched, guttural and scraping, like metal against stone: the Out-Dweller's breathing.

Melanie shrank back against the wall and found she could not breathe. Could not think, at least not of anything but flight. This was not a thing she could face and live. It would rip her very soul from her corpse and feed on it for all eternity.

Run, you stupid ninny. Run!

Somehow, she did not. Some part of her was certain that if she did, if she moved at all from that spot, the beast would detect her, chase her down, and then... She would have shuddered except she could not bring herself to move even that much.

The Out-Dweller growled, a deep basso that carried entire volumes of rage and hatred, then took another step forward.

And stumbled.

In a flash, Melanie realized why it had stopped in the first place. It was standing on the edge of Loran's warding. Had in fact pushed itself past the warding, and been hampered by it.

The Inquisitor went up quite a bit in her estimation. She knew beyond a doubt there was nothing she could have done to make such a being pause, let alone lose its feet.

Brilliant white light, more bright than the sun at noon, lanced out from the top of the stairs alongside the sisters' building and struck the Out-Dweller in the chest. The world exploded in a rainbow of light and the Out-Dweller's scream was only eclipsed by Melanie's own as she cowered back from the sudden assault.

More bellows and screams, and deeper sounds that more resembled the groans of a building about to give way than those of a living creature followed, and that was all Melanie could sense for a long moment. After-images of Loran's attack dominated her vision, leaving only a purple-white blob in front of her for what seemed an eternity.

The smell of smoke and burning flesh filled the air and the Out-Dweller stomped a foot down, or at least that was what it sounded like. A man's voice cried out. She could not make out who.

Melanie blinked her eyes quickly and turned her head away, trying to clear her vision.

Another bellow, this one from the beast again. Then the concussion of a detonation - from a fireball, by the sound of it.

Something struck her chest and Melanie was knocked back against the wall for a small eternity. The force constricted her and she could not breathe. Could not move. Could not see, though that was hardly anything new.

Then, all at once, the force was gone and she collapsed to the ground on her belly, gasping.

Still the battle went on, and from the sound of things it was not going well. Booms, growls, shouts, grunts, little explosions... Enough that it seemed she had been on the ground for hours.

But when she managed to push herself up to her hands and knees and raise her head to look, it was plain that only a few seconds had passed. Loran was advancing down the stairs, his staff clasped in both hands, one end of the staff shining like a little star. He wore an expression of grim determination despite the cut on his forehead and his disheveled hair. Raedrick lay on his back to the right, where he had apparently been thrown by the force that had knocked Melanie down, and was just now raising himself up onto his elbows. Julian was nowhere in sight.

The Out-Dweller reared up to its full height, easily ten feet if not a couple more, and the shadows ringing it whipped and whirled like tentacles. Tentacles that ended in scythes. Loran ducked beneath one, and it cut cleanly through the stairs above and behind him, sending them falling to the ground with a clatter.

The Inquisitor yelled a battle-cry in a tongue Melanie did not recognize - and she knew many - and leapt off the stairs to his right, dropping the dozen feet or so to land on the ground in the alley between the sisters' building and its neighbor. As he landed, a series of starlets, smaller versions of the brilliant beam that was his initial attack, shot from the end of his staff and flew at the Out-Dweller.

The beast growled again and moved its right arm. Tendrils of blackness whipped around in front of it and intercepted the starlets, one by one.

Loran snarled and took a step forward, barking out another incantation. A second series of starlets flew forth, more numerous this time.

Again whirling black tendrils reached out to intercept them, but this time the starlets were too many, and two struck home.

The Out-Dweller hissed and stumbled backward a half-step, looking for a moment as though it would fall completely. But instead it found its footing and rose upright once more, bounding forward toward the Inquisitor.

Loran's lips compressed and he thrust his staff out before himself.

A hemisphere of translucent blue energy appeared in front of the Out-Dweller, stopping it in its advance. The beast howled and pressed its arms forward against the barrier, rage at the minuscule rodent that was trying to thwart it evident from the way its eyes flashed.

Loran leaned forward against his staff as though it was a physical wall, and he cried out an incantation of force. Melanie recognized the spell at once: it had been among the first spells Timon taught her. For a second, she was surprised Loran would use that one; it was elementary. But then, the earliest teachings are often those learned the best, and against an onslaught like the one the Out-Dweller was bringing he would need something he knew instinctively and was very, *very* good at.

The Out-Dweller reeled backward as Loran's spell hit it, and again it looked as though it was going to go over onto its back. But as before it righted itself, and it pushed back.

Hard.

Loran was leaning against his staff like a man bracing a wall that was about to fall over. His feet were planted firmly against the dirt of the alley and, as the Out-Dweller came forward, he again shouted out the force incantation at the top of his lungs.

He may as well have tried to hold back the tide.

The Inquisitor moved backwards. Slowly at first, then more quickly as the Out-Dweller gained momentum. Loran's feet dug furrows into the dirt of the alley and he grimaced against the beast's onslaught.

Then the Out-Dweller bellowed, far louder than anything it had voiced to this point, and gave a great shove forward.

Loran flew bodily backwards through the air, losing his grip on his staff as he flew, and landed on his back ten feet from where he stood a second before. He hit the ground hard and did not move.

The Out-Dweller raised its head and howled in victory to the midnight sky above, then, slowly, implacably, it began to advance.

Melanie forced herself to her feet and reached into her belt pouch, watching the beast's advance through narrowed eyes.

And also watching Loran.

The Inquisitor stirred, moving sluggishly, like a man dazed - and small wonder - as he tried to push himself up to a seated position.

This was her chance for revenge. If she let the Out-Dweller do it, she would never have the satisfaction. She reached down into the belt pouch and pulled out the components for Timon's favorite offensive spell. The one she had to pay all manner of carnal prices to get him to teach. Prices that she was all too happy to pay, but prices nonetheless.

From off to the left, a figure emerged out of the shadows and raced forward. Lamplight and moonlight joined together to reflect off Julian's sword as he cut at the beast's quarter.

The Out-Dweller flicked its left hand contemptuously, like a man swatting at a midge, and a tendril of darkness whipped around and knocked Julian on his left temple. He fell in a heap.

Red-hot rage, and the shock of feared loss, threatened to intrude on the cold calm that Melanie had surrounded herself with. Her nemesis lay on the ground, helpless. She might never get this chance again.

But you couldn't take this thing on your own if you tried, and it's responsible for the murders.

She growled at herself and forced the little voice in her head away.

It will kill again and it will be all your fault.

So what? Timon, the love of her life, was dead. Dead in the most horrific way possible, and the man responsible was lying vulnerable at her feet, just waiting for her vengeance.

On the ground in front of her, Julian rolled over and raised his head. For a moment, their eyes met and she saw his lips moving. He shook his head in denial.

Melanie began her incantation and Julian's face became obscured behind the flames that flared up around her outstretched hands.

❧ 23 ❧

THROWING DOWN

The Out-Dweller advanced toward Loran, who was lying helpless on the ground.

Julian screamed at himself to move, to take action in this fight which could determine the future for his town, but found he could not.

Ever since the Out-Dweller appeared, he had been in a near panic. Nothing he had ever faced could have prepared him for this. The Out-Dweller's physical presence was enough to cow him. But more than that, he felt a weight on his mind, a crushing force that strove to drive him to his knees, and it took every ounce of energy he had to stop himself from doing just that.

He watched, immobile, as Loran attacked and Raedrick rushed to support the mage, but was repelled without even half a thought.

He wanted to help. He wanted to desperately. But he could. Not. Make. Himself. Move.

Little Stars flashed across his vision from the left, and a couple of them struck the Out-Dweller.

That just seemed to make it mad.

The beast came on, and pushed Loran's force-shield—or whatever it was—aside like it was so much rubbish. The mage went flying, and Julian hung his head.

It was over.

They had failed.

Then, off to his right, he saw movement. He glanced that way and stopped, staring, as Melanie pushed herself to her feet. Where had she come from? Wherever it was, she looked ready for a fight. A fierce fire lit up her eyes.

Julian looked at that raging fire and drew strength from it. This was the thing that had been accosting his people these many days. It had taken good people from their families, for its own foul amusement.

He looked back at the Out-Dweller as it stalked toward Loran's collapsed form and let the rage he saw in Melanie's eyes flow through him. He would not let this foul thing win.

He. Would. Not.

Crying out, Julian ripped his sword from its scabbard and bounded forward.

The small of the Out-Dweller's back was right in front of him. An easy target, one that would put the thing on its knees where the mages could take it down without any more trouble.

Something hit him on the side of the head, something that felt like six war hammers bundled together, and sent him reeling.

He hit the ground and all he could see for a long moment were flashing spots in front of his eyes. All he could smell was the Out-Dweller's rotten stink. All he could taste was the mud of the side street. Not that anything in Lydelton was *not* a side street, but still.

After a moment, he raised his head, and saw Melanie.

She was on her feet, a righteous fury in her eyes and a look on her face that he had seen a hundred times in a dozen battles. The look of someone ready to kill, without remorse.

The elation of impending victory leapt into him, but then he turned his head to follow her gaze. She was not looking at the Out-Dweller. She was looking at Loran.

By the Gods, she had chosen *now* to get her vengeance? She was going to kill them all!

"No!" he screamed, as loud as he could, looking back at Melanie in desperation.

Melanie's eyes locked onto his for a second and he thought she understood, then she looked away and began waving her arms around as she began a spell incantation. Flames sprouted out around both her hands, as though from nowhere, then she raised both hands.

A column of flame, as thick around as Julian's thigh, lanced out from Melanie's hands.

And struck the Out-Dweller in the center of its back.

The Out-Dweller bellowed in obvious pain as the fire billowed around its torso and engulfed it in a ball of living flame that encased it and burned its flesh from all sides. The beast spun a full circle and howled in agony, raising its head to the sky as it gave voice to its pain.

To Julian's left, Loran raised himself to his elbows, his eyebrows climbing high onto his forehead in surprise as the Out-Dweller was stymied. The mage wasted no time though. He rolled to his right, gathering up his staff mid-roll, and came up on one knee, the end of his staff pointing toward the stricken beast.

Miniature stars, the same things that had before harried the Out-Dweller, raced from Loran's staff and impacted the beast in its arms, legs, head...everywhere that was not covered by Melanie's fire.

The Out-Dweller screamed again, then turned away from Loran and ran. It fled past Julian, and he had to flatten himself beneath the heat of Melanie's flames as much as from the frenzied flailing of the Out-Dweller's shadow-tentacles, or whatever they were.

Melanie threw her hands up as the beast fled past her, and the flames winked out of existence, but the Out-Dweller continued running, its howls louder than the loudest thunder as it fled Lydelton.

All around, windows began lighting up as townsfolk, roused from their sleep by the sound of the battle, lit lamps. Chagrined shouts began echoing down the street as people threw up their sashes and inquired of their neighbors as to what was going on. Others began pouring out of their houses, looking around for the source of the disturbance.

Julian ignored them, pushing himself to his feet and walking over toward Melanie.

She stood with her arms limp at her sides, her eyes dazed as though she could not believe what had just happened. Julian could not blame her.

"Melanie?" he said. "Are you al..."

Loran's shout, filled with righteous indignation, interrupted his thought. "You!"

Julian turn to see the mage on his feet, advancing toward Melanie with his staff lowered, the end that had just shot starlets at the Out-Dweller pointed right at her.

"I should have known it was you!" Loran stalked closer, his snarl fitting a lion about to strike. "I always suspected..." He trailed off into a furious growl, and the end of his staff crackled with little bits of lightning.

Julian fell back a half-step and raised his hands defensively. "Whoa!" he said. "Loran, wait..."

Again he was cut off, this time by Melanie. Looking aside at her, she stood erect, facing Loran. Her eyes flashed with that same rage Julian saw earlier, and she had raised her hands before herself again in a defensive posture. The fact that her hands were again wreathed in flame lent entire volumes to the weight that posture gave.

"I *always* knew," Melanie said, her tone as withering as the flames she had just shot from her hands. "You killed Timon, and you loved doing it."

Her eyes widened even more and the flames around her hands grew until they almost eclipsed her face.

Aw hell. They were going to throw down right here.

Before he realized what he was doing, Julian leapt between the two of them, his hands raised, one palm facing each of them. "Whoa there," he said. "Stop!"

Loran's staff blazed with barely-contained energy, matching Melanie's flames in its incandescence. All of a sudden, Julian realized he had just done an incredibly stupid thing.

"Get out of the way, Julian," Melanie said from his left, through clenched teeth.

From his right, Loran added, "Yes, Constable, do move. It would be unfortunate if I harmed you while taking this abomination to ground."

Julian blinked, unable to believe what he had just heard Loran say. Suddenly Melanie's hands were not the only things burning with sudden fury. He turned on Loran. "Abomination?" he said, more like shouted. "This abomination," he pointed back at Melanie, "Just saved your sorry ass from that thing. Or hadn't you noticed?"

Loran's scowl only deepened. He did not reply, but the energy around his staff grew more bright.

Julian wanted to cringe, to duck, anything to avoid being turned into a charcoal briquette by the two mages. But he could not do any of those things. Not without sacrificing his dignity, and at the same time giving them leave to throw down on each other.

They stood there, tension so thick you could eat it with a spoon, for an eternity.

Then Raedrick, standing behind Loran and to his left, cleared his throat. "Might want to take a look around you, Magester," Julian's friend said.

Loran turned his head slightly to look at Raedrick, then his eyes widened and he panned his head around, taking in the scene.

Julian did the same.

All around, townsfolk stood, knives, shovels, and the occasional sword or bow - retrieved from the attic, no doubt - in hand. They stood in a loose circle around the two mages, weapons, makeshift or not, at the ready.

"You might want to rethink things, Loran," Raedrick said. "See, Melanie here saved this town and everyone in it. These people would much rather have her around than the likes of you."

A few men raised cudgels and smacked them into their palms in strident counterpoint to Raedrick's statement.

Loran's brow furrowed, and for a moment Julian thought he was going to rain down holy hell on the lot of them, and to blazes with the consequences.

Then, slowly, the mage nodded. He lowered his staff, and the crackling energy that had been gathering at its end dissipated and went out.

"I suppose a bit of negotiation is in order," Loran said.

That was the understatement of the year.

❧ 24 ❧

UNLIKELY ALLIES

"We don't have much time."

Julian found it hard to argue with Loran's statement, but all the same his words, and more in particular his tone, made Julian want to punch him.

"Speak for yourself," he said, glancing around at the ring of men surrounding them. "I have all the time in the world, Magester." He added a bit of contempt to the last word, just because.

Loran quirked an eyebrow at him, then turned his gaze toward Melanie. "The Out-Dweller gets further away by the moment, my lady." The "my lady" contained all manner of derision. "We can track it for a time, but that time is not indefinite."

Melanie looked confused.

Loran smirked ever so slightly. "Oh, you cannot track it? I'm so sorry." He looked away from her, disdainfully, toward Raedrick. "Is this," he gestured toward Melanie, "half-trained and mostly ignorant harlot really worth risking your town for, Constable?"

Melanie's eyes grew wide and she drew herself up, inhaling deeply through her nose.

Raedrick raised a hand toward her, ordering calm from his demeanor and expression alone. For a moment, Julian thought

Melanie would ignore him and go for Loran's throat anyway. But she surprised him and exhaled deeply, shaking her hands at her sides to let the frustration Julian knew she contained loose.

"Get to the point, Magester," Readrick said. His tone was bland, but from the wrinkles around his eyes, Julian could see he was about ready to rip Loran's throat out himself.

Loran snorted disdainfully. "I am willing to let your alliance with this...thing...go unreported, Constable." Loran clearly did not know who he was talking to. Or rather, he did not know Raedrick enough to recognize the warning signs. Julian was hardly surprised at all when he just kept on going, digging his own grave. "But you must understand I have an obligation to bring her back with me to face justice."

Raedrick's nostrils flared almost as much as Melanie's did. Julian had to lay a restraining hand on her arm to keep her in check. He was not able to do the same with his friend.

In a flash, Raedrick's sword was out of its scabbard. The mage tried to retreat, but Raedrick grabbed Loran's right shoulder with his left hand and held him close, pressing the edge of the blade into Loran's throat. The mage's skin wrinkled beneath the sword's steel; just a hair's breadth more pressure and it would draw blood.

And Loran knew it. His eyes widened in shock. In fear.

Raedrick spoke very softly, very firmly. "Melanie is not a thing," he said. "Not an abomination. She is my friend, and you will not have her. Ever." He drew a deep breath and seemed to calm himself a bit. "We need your help, Magester," he said, and released the mage, giving the slight man a little shove away from him. "And you need ours. We will track this Out-Dweller back to its master with you. You will get your fugitive. But then you leave us in peace." Raedrick's brow furrowed and his voice took on a dangerous tone. "And you will never tell your people about Melanie. Ever."

Loran looked spooked. It was the first time Julian had ever seen him that way. He raised his fingers to his throat and felt along the area Raedrick's sword had touched, then pulled them away and looked at them as though expecting blood. Seeing none, his shoulders slumped. But his eyes still burned with pride.

"You are in no position to dictate terms, Constable," he said, spitting out the title with all the contempt he could muster. "The Magestirium has authority over matters magical, not - "

"Not here," Raedrick finished. "Not with her."

Loran glowered and looked away from Raedrick toward Julian.

Julian put on his best scowl and let his sword-hand fall onto the hilt of his weapon.

The mage sniffed and scanned the faces of the men surrounding them. They were all as implacable as Julian felt, and as Raedrick looked. Finally, Loran nodded.

"Fine. She goes free," he said. Then, raising his index finger, he added, "For now. But if she puts her foot wrong with the Magestirium again, or sets foot outside of this Vale..." He left the rest unsaid.

Raedrick nodded. "Agreed. Melanie?" He looked at her, questioning.

Melanie shrugged. "Didn't intend to go anywhere else anyway."

"Then we have an accord," Loran said. He rolled his shoulders and turned away from Raedrick, in the direction the Out-Dweller fled. He took a step, but the circle of townsfolk did not give way. Loran looked back at Raedrick, an eyebrow quirking upward again. "Do you mind?"

Raedrick nodded at the townsfolk, and the circle opened, letting Loran pass.

The mage departed, hurrying down the street after the Out-Dweller.

Julian looked at Raedrick questioningly. "You believe him?"

Raedrick shrugged. "If he's lying, we can kill him later."

Chuckling, Julian joined his friend as he followed along behind Loran. The game was afoot, after all.

❦ 25 ❦

PURSUIT

It was a half-block before Julian realized that Melanie was jogging along with them. And then only because she caught up to them and threatened to pass him up.

"You sure you want to come with us?" he said between breaths.

She rolled her eyes. "You'll all die if you go up against that thing without me," she said. "And then I'll have to clean up your mess. Of course I'm coming."

Julian would have chuckled, but the pace precluded it. Instead he just grinned at her. She returned it in kind, but the smile did not reach her eyes, which looked haunted. Pained.

"Are you going to be ok?"

Melanie flinched slightly, but her stride did not alter. She nodded quickly, but said nothing more.

Julian left it at that.

They jogged along after Loran, who turned through the streets of Lydelton seemingly at random but presumably following the Out-Dweller's trail toward its, or rather its master's, hideout.

"I thought you said the warding would weaken it enough so Julian and I could take it alone," Raedrick said, a question in his tone.

Loran managed a little shrug as he jogged. "I had not realized how powerful it is. It appears to be a Lord of one of the dark planes. They are," he paused for a breath and, Julian thought, for emphasis, "Formidable."

They ran on.

"Why doesn't it just go back to where it came from?" Julian asked after the third turn. "Why run away like this?"

Melanie opened her mouth to reply but Loran cut her off.

"Because it was summoned," the mage said. "It can only enter or leave this world from the place it was summoned."

Loran did not look back at them as he answered. He had not looked back at all. Julian would bet good money he did not know Melanie was with them. He was in for a shock. Julian could not help grinning at the thought.

"So if we kill it here, away from its place of summoning?" Raedrick asked.

"It dies. Forever." Loran's voice held a certain satisfaction as he answered.

Wow. That was something Julian did not know. Although if he was honest with himself, the things he did not know could fill an entire library. All the same, he had always been taught that the denizens of the outer planes were immortal. Un-aging, undying. Even if you killed one of them, the legends said he would just regenerate and be ready to come after you again. But apparently that only applied on their home planes. If an Out-Dweller could truly die here, in the real world...

"No wonder they don't come here very often," Julian said aloud.

"Indeed," Loran replied. Then he turned right down a cross street.

"This street will take us out of town," Raedrick said.

Loran just shrugged and jogged on.

Sure enough, they passed the last houses of Lydelton proper, and shortly thereafter the street ended in the face of the tall grass that dominated most of Glimmer Vale during the warm months. Except that tonight, there was a path beaten through the grass. Half again as wide as the broadest man Julian had ever met, it led away from town to the north, toward the eastern-most edges of the Glamorwood and the hills and mountains beyond.

Loran pulled up short, panting heavily. He bent forward and rested his hands upon his knees, catching his breath. Part of Julian wanted to do the same, but he would not allow himself to mimic the mage's lack of conditioning, so instead he worked hard to keep himself upright. He took in long breaths and forcibly held them in to make it look as though he was not winded. That did not do much as far as getting his breath back, but it made him feel better.

For his part, Loran took several moments before he straightened. He looked back at Raedrick and Julian, then noticed Melanie and he scowled.

"I did not invite *you*, woman," he said, applying all manner of derision to the word woman as he spoke it.

"And yet here I am anyway, Vigilant Haversted," Melanie said calmly. She was not breathing heavily at all, curse her. "We both know you will need my help to prevail this night."

Loran scowled at her for a long moment. Then he looked away, saying nothing more.

"Enough," Raedrick said. He was not winded in the slightest, Julian noticed. He made a mental note to join Raedrick on his daily runs from then on. "Let's finish this."

Raedrick set off through the grass, his shoulders set in the determined manner Julian knew so well. It was kill or be killed now, until one side or the other prevailed.

"Right," Julian said. "Let's get to it." Then he followed his friend into the grass.

The trail was easy enough to follow, even in the dim light of the stars and the crescent moon, now low over the eastern hills as she got ready to lay down her burden for the day. Not that her burden was all that large at this time of year, but Julian supposed her longer rest now made up for her greater burden at other times, when she had to shine the entire night through and some of the day as well.

As opposed to the Out-Dweller's course through town, the trail through the grass ran straight enough that Julian could have set his compass to it. Never once did the thing deviate from its track northward. It just continued on, and the mountains ahead of them slowly loomed closer, darker bits of darkness that slowly blotted out more stars as their little group drew nearer.

"Does this make sense to you?" Julian asked after a half-hour following the trail deeper into the wilderness. "Why would it run straight like this?" That question had been bugging him for the last quarter mile, and it just irked him more with every step.

"It presumes we lost its trail in the town," Loran said, again without looking back at Julian.

Julian stopped. "No way this thing is that stupid." Melanie stopped beside him.

Raedrick looked over at Julian and frowned, then slowed his steps and stopped as well.

Something was not right here.

Loran was not to be dissuaded, though. "It is injured, and needs to retreat to its home," he said, finally slowing to look back at them.

Just then, something reared out of the grass ahead of them and to the right, just past Loran's shoulder. A sickly sweet, rotten scent swept over them as it moved, a scent Julian recognized instantly.

The Out-Dweller.

"Get down," Julian and Raedrick yelled together, even as they both drew their blades and charged forward.

Melanie beat them both. They had not gone more than two

steps before her hands again lit up with the fire. She raised both hands and fire lanced out over Julian's head - good thing he had decided to run at a crouch - toward the beast.

But the fire struck nothing. It just flew away into the night for several seconds before Melanie raised her hands and shut the flames off. Julian looked at her and noticed she was clenching her fists tightly; was that how she controlled it?

"It's still out there," Melanie said, cocking her head sideways, listening.

Julian did the same, and found that he could hear it too. Low, almost too low to register, but it was there. A rhythmic thumping. It was impossible to tell which direction it came from; it seemed to emanate from everywhere. He turned a complete circle, squinting out into the blackness, and flexed his fingers on the grip of his sword. Nothing.

"I don't like this," he said.

Raedrick grunted in reply, and that grunt carried entire levels of agreement.

The Out-Dweller's sound grew louder, as though it was getting closer. And then, abruptly, it stopped.

Silence reigned. Even the usual night insects were missing.

"I like this even less."

No sooner had the words left Julian's mouth than the silence was eclipsed by a roar that put the Silver Falls to shame. Waves of sound rolled over them, striking against them in a physical blow that sent Julian and his companions to their knees. He reflexively covered his ears with his hands as he went down, but it did no good. The sound came on and on, hammering him again and again until he lay rolled in a ball on the ground.

He ached all over from the pummeling, his ears rang intensely, and he felt like he would never be able to move again.

Several seconds of lying like that before Julian realized that the onslaught of noise had ceased.

Or had it?

He pushed himself up to a sitting position and tried to say something to Loran, who lay sprawled next to him. But again all he could hear was the ringing in his ears; he could not even hear himself speak, the ringing was so loud.

This was bad. Very bad.

He had dropped his sword somewhere. Frantically he looked around for it. All around, his companions were slowly beginning to come to their senses, but they were not doing it fast enough.

There. He snatched up his sword and forced himself to his feet.

Just in time to see two pairs of gleaming red orbs approaching from within a shadow deeper than the blackest night.

Bugger me, he tried to say, though deafened as he was he could not be sure how it came out.

The Out-Dweller was at most twenty feet away, moving quickly.

Julian kicked Loran with the back of his boot and then advanced. Every part of his sane mind screamed at him to run the other way; he could not win this one. But this time that part of him did not come close to taking control. It was one thing to take no action while others could. It was something else entirely to flee while leaving your friends helpless.

Ok, Loran did not count as a friend. But for this night, at least, he was an ally, and that amounted to the same thing.

He stumbled as he advanced, suddenly realizing he did not have his equilibrium fully.

The darkness around the Out-Dweller swirled forward like a whip aimed at Julian's head, but passed over him. Had he not stumbled right then, he had no doubt the thing would have taken his head clean off.

Another tendril of black came at him, visible only because it was darker than the night around it.

Julian threw himself forward into a roll, hoping against hope that he had guessed right about the thing's trajectory but bracing himself in case he had not.

Again a miss. Somehow.

He came out of the roll and up to his feet. Mostly. And had to fling himself back to the ground and shield his eyes as the sun - or rather suns, dozens of them - flew through the air past him and into the darkness of the Out-Dweller's body.

The beast drew back. Julian presumed it roared, but even that mighty noise could not penetrate the ringing in his ears. He looked over his shoulder and saw Loran up on his knees, his staff in his hands.

Then another burst of stars flew from the staff, and all Julian could see for several long seconds were purple after-images.

The ground shook. Once. Twice.

Something hot flashed briefly overtop him.

And then all was still. Not silent; his ears still rang loudly. But still.

Just raised his head and looked around.

Loran stood leaning against his staff. Melanie was on one knee a short distance away, her hands aglow with flame. Raedrick remained on the ground. Dread flowed through Julian to see that. He pushed himself to his feet and stumbled over to his friend.

Or tried to. He fell back to his knees before he could go more than a yard.

Damn it!

Julian called out Raedrick's name, futilely. The others were likely no better at hearing that he was at the moment. But that did not matter. Raedrick needed help.

Julian pushed himself back to his hands and knees and crawled over to where Raedrick lay. The other man was sprawled on his back, his left arm bent at an unnatural angle from its shoulder. He eyes were closed, and in the flickering light of Melanie's fire Julian could not tell if he was breathing or not.

Julian reached out and shook his friend's shoulder.

Raedrick's entire body stiffened and he jerked up to a sitting position, his mouth wide as though he were shouting. Again, nothing but ringing in Julian's ears, but that did not matter. Right then, he was so happy to see his friend moving he did not mind one bit.

Julian grinned broadly. Raedrick replied with a grimace, and a look that could kill at fifteen paces.

He probably should have shook the other shoulder.

❧ 26 ☙

FIRST AID

The immediate aftermath of the Out-Dweller's attack would have been pure chaos had there been more than four of them in the grass. As it was, it was confusion that Julian would have found tremendously amusing in any other circumstances. But being in the wide open, in the middle of the night, with a large and apparently very angry other-worldly beast stalking around was not the right time for humor.

None of them could hear anything; or at least Julian presumed the others were as deafened as he was from their hand gestures and annoyed faces. Thus, it took a while for everyone to agree on the priority of tasks. Namely, making more light - how could they have been stupid enough to go running through the grass without bringing some light with them? - and seeing to Raedrick's shoulder.

Loran accomplished the light easily enough. He grimaced, stood to his full height - not that that was saying much - and mumbled something that Julian was sure he would not have understood even if he were not still deafened, and thumped his staff against the ground. A small sphere, glowing blue-white and brighter than twenty lamps held together, rose from the top of his staff and came to hover about ten feet over his head.

That illuminated things quite nicely.

Raedrick's shoulder took a bit more doing. Julian had seen similar injuries before; the shoulder joint was...dislocated, he thought the medics called it. He had seen a pair of them fix a fellow who had been hurt similarly. It required one of them holding the man steady and the other giving his arm a great jerk to set it in place. It seemed to hurt the poor fellow a lot, but after a few minutes, he was swinging his arm around almost like new.

Julian tried, using only gestures, to pass along what they would have to do and received only a blank stare and raised eyebrow from Melanie. Raedrick nodded; he had seen it done as well. Loran...

Loran could not be bothered to help. He looked down at Julian, Raedrick, and Melanie and sniffed, then looked away, out into the night.

Anger surged through Julian for a moment, then faded just as quickly. The mage had a point. They could not all tend to Raedrick. *Someone* needed to keep an eye out in case the Out-Dweller came back. Better he did it than, say Julian. He would be more effective against the beast, and anyway, Julian doubted he had the muscle to do what needed doing.

It made sense. It was still more than irritating.

Slowly, very slowly, in the midst of all that, the ringing in Julian's ears faded. It did not vanish completely, but it reduced, little by little until he could finally hear the others' occasional grunt or murmured curse of annoyance - no doubt uttered because they believed no one else could hear. Julian did not realize it had happened until, after Loran refused to take a hand with getting Raedrick's shoulder in place, Melanie let loose a particularly colorful remark about his heritage.

He couldn't help it. Julian started to chuckle.

Melanie looked at him, crossly. "What are you laughing at..." She stopped abruptly, and her eyebrows rose high on her head as she smiled. In relief, if she felt at all like Julian did.

They exchanged grins, and Julian could not help but notice

how the blue-white light from Loran's spell made her eyes seem to glow.

A long moment passed, in silence.

Raedrick cleared his throat. "A little help here?"

Melanie gave a little start. Julian felt his cheeks go warm and he coughed into his fist.

"Right," he said. "This is going to hurt..."

"I know that." Raedrick was already speaking through clenched teeth. It hurt already. Obviously.

Julian gave him an apologetic half-smile - the most he could muster right then - which Raedrick returned with a roll of his eyes and an impatient grunt.

Melanie placed her hands on Raedrick's good shoulder and the meat of his neck on the injured side, being careful to keep clear of the shoulder joint itself.

"Ok," Julian said. He took hold of Raedrick's arm just above the elbow and placed his other hand on his shoulder. His fingers touched Melanie's, and for the briefest of moments his thoughts lingered on the softness of her skin.

Enough of that.

He took a deep breath and looked Raedrick in the eye. "Ready?"

Raedrick nodded.

"One."

Julian tightened his grip on his friend's arm.

"Two"

Raedrick drew a deep breath.

"Three."

Julian pushed Raedrick's arm upwards into its shoulder socket with all the force he could muster.

Raedrick cried out. Loudly. Very loudly. For a second, Julian wondered that his ears did not start ringing the way they had after the Out-Dweller attacked with sound, as loudly as he screamed.

And then, a moment later, it was over.

Julian released his friend and backed away. Melanie did the same.

Very slowly, Raedrick rolled his shoulder, wincing the whole way. "That..." he said, breathlessly, "was horrible."

"But did it work?" Melanie was all business in her tone, though her eyes showed her concern as she looked at him.

Raedrick gave his shoulder another couple rolls, then moved his arm back and forth a couple times. He nodded. "Think so. For the time being, anyway."

Relief flooded through Julian and he grinned from ear to ear. He stood and offered Raedrick a hand up. "Better have the healing house take a look at it when we get back, anyway," he said. "Just in case."

Raedrick accept the hand up - he used his sword hand, which was uninjured. "Oh, I will." He got to his feet then took a moment to retrieve his sword and re-sheathe it. Then he turned his gaze, all business again, toward Loran. "Well Magester? Do you know where it went?"

Loran was peering off to the northeast, into the grass away from the Out-Dweller's trail. He did not turn his head when Raedrick addressed him. He just looked at Julian's friend from the corner of his eye, and nodded. "It has moved away again."

"You can still track it?"

Loran nodded again. "The trail is fresh."

"Then let's get to it."

ON THE TRAIL

There was a brief debate over what to do with Loran's sphere of light, but in the end they opted to keep it lit. The Out-Dweller already knew they were there, and presumably its master, the fugitive, would find out as soon as it communicated with him again. Given that, thoughts of stealth lost out over the necessity of seeing their surroundings, the better to not be ambushed again.

They set off.

Almost immediately, the Out-Dweller's trail left the beaten path through the grass, veering more northeast than north. Julian presumed they would encounter another beaten path at some point, but after a quarter hour or so, by his best reckoning, it appeared that was not to be the case.

"It really was quite clever," Melanie said, from where she walked to Julian's left.

"Huh?"

She rolled her eyes and gave him a look of reproach. "That other path. The Out-Dweller must have laid it as a lure, a ploy to get us to go where it wanted."

He had not thought of that, but it made sense. He should have seen it before. He shook his head and let out a disgusted snort. "And we fell for it, like fools."

Ahead of them, Loran glanced back over his shoulder. "Never presume that an Out-Dweller is not cunning. Even some of the highest-ranking members of the Magestirium have been fooled by such as them." He paused, then added. "From time to time."

He went back to focusing on the way ahead, and Melanie...stuck her tongue out at his back.

Julian gaped at her, shock over her action rendering him speechless for a long moment.

Melanie looked sidelong at him. "What?" she said, in a low tone of voice that was meant for Julian's ears alone. "He was taken in just like the rest of us." She lowered her voice in a mocking imitation of Loran's voice. "Even members of the Magestirium have been fooled." She snorted. "Arrogant twit."

Julian laughed, more loudly than he meant to. Raedrick shot him a withering look from ahead, next to Loran, and made a shushing gesture.

Julian clamped his mouth shut, but still found himself chortling for a good several minutes, try though he might to stop.

It ended up not being an issue. In the darkness ahead, the mountains loomed higher and higher, blotting out more of the stars. Gradually, Julian realized that the gently rolling terrain of the grassland had changed, becoming more steep and varied.

They had entered the hills at the foot of the mountains.

Loran brought them to a halt atop a rise, the steepest one they had yet traversed, and Julian was struck by a memory from when he and Raedrick first arrived in Lydelton. They had tried to track one of Isenholf's brigands back to their base, at night. That had not worked out very well, he recalled.

Of course, they were not following a magical trail, or scent, or whatever it was that Loran was able to detect from the Out-Dweller.

"Still on top of it?" Julian asked.

The mage nodded curtly, then raised his staff and pointed directly north. "The beast passed by here not twenty minutes ago."

"We're gaining on it?" They had taken at least that long to recover their hearing, square away Raedrick's shoulder, and get moving again, by Julian's way of reckoning.

Loran made a noncommittal gesture with his free hand. "We've been keeping pace the last mile or two." He frowned. "It's as though the beast is not trying to lose us." He turned a concerned gaze on all of them. "Like it wants us to follow it to its lair."

Raedrick grunted. "That can't be good."

"No, I should think not." Loran gathered himself up and gave them a curt little nod. "Let's go."

The trail led down the hilltop where they stopped and then ran to the left, northward, in the small valley created by a trio of nearby hills. Again Julian was struck by the similarity with the brigand incident, and he found himself wondering whether the Out-Dweller and its master, or whatever their relationship was, were encamped in another one of those things the brigands had used. What was it Melanie called it? He could not recall.

Julian shook his head at his own foolishness. No way there were two of those things here in Glimmer Vale, not as rare as Melanie said they were. If so few mages could do it...

Wait a second.

"Melanie," he said. "I thought you said there were only a few men in the entire world who could make one of those plane things."

She quirked an eyebrow at him.

"You know, the between-plane-whatever-you-called it."

She smirked at him. "You mean a trans-planar rift?"

He nodded.

"They are exceedingly difficult to make. Only a very few have the skill."

"So this guy, this fugitive, is one of the most powerful mages in the world, if he can do that." Julian swallowed and looked around at the hills on either side of them, suddenly quite a bit more nervous. "How are we supposed to take someone like that down?"

Loran must have overheard because he broke in, his voice thick with disapproval. "You speak of what you do not know, Constable. We are not dealing with a rift, but a summoning." Loran shot a withering look at Melanie, the kind of look that said, "Why are you even talking about this with these ignorant louts, woman?"

Julian found that look a bit amusing, actually. She was already an outlaw in the Magestirium's eyes. Was she really supposed to keep all their secrets, despite that?

For her part, Melanie merely sniffed at the mage's look.

"What's the difference?" Raedrick asked.

Loran gave him a perturbed look, and for a moment Julian thought sure he was not going to answer. Normal people should not meddle in the affairs of Wizards, as some very pretentious mages - and that was saying something - who were stationed with the Army had taken to calling themselves around post.

But Loran surprised him. "A trans-planar rift is a connection between one plane and another. A boring through reality to create a passage. The energy requirements for that sort of work are tremendous, and the required control so fine, that one can easily study for a lifetime and still not develop the skill required to create one successfully."

He paused, quirking his head to one side for a moment. Then he nodded and changed course to the right, veering sidelong up one of the hills. "This way."

They turned to follow him. Loran grunted and stepped around a protruding rock before continuing. "A summoning is merely an invitation. The summoner calls out the creature's name and imbues it with power, usually using a summoning circle. The rite creates," he paused as though searching for the right word, "a thinning in the boundary to our plane. If the creature being summoned accepts the invitation, it then creates a temporary rift to that thinning."

Julian blinked. "It can refuse to come?"

Loran shrugged. "If the summoned creature is powerful enough, or the mage lacking in skill. For a man who is learned and practiced in these things, a summoning is closer to a command for any but the most powerful of beings. For beings like that, it is more...a negotiation."

"That means this particular Out-Dweller *wants* to be here," Raedrick mused.

Loran nodded. "Almost certainly." He smirked then, in a rather self-satisfied way. "Or at least, it *did*."

Don't throw your arm out of joint patting yourself on the back, Magester. Julian snorted.

"So how do we get rid of it?" Raedrick frowned as he asked the question. "Besides killing it, if we even can."

Loran shrugged. "Break the summoning circle. Kill the summoner. Perform a banishing ceremony at the place it was summoned. There are many ways." He drew a deep breath. "I am hoping," he said, "that I will be able to convince my former colleague to surrender, and break the summoning himself."

Yeah, like that was going to happen. "And when he doesn't?"

Loran looked at Julian, scowling. Then, after a brief moment, he relaxed his expression and sighed, looking resigned. "Then it becomes...more difficult."

Great.

They reached the crest of the hill and Loran slowed, looking left and right. Finally, he turned left and strode down the other side briskly, his gait businesslike and his shoulders squared like a man setting off for a long day of hard labor.

Julian looked up from the mage, toward the twinkling stars above. But before his eyes could reach them, another twinkling, faint but bright enough to draw his attention in the night's darkness, drew his attention. Yellow-orange, the light flickered fitfully and it took a short while for him to realize what he was looking at.

A campfire. Or if not a campfire, a fire of some sort. And either unshielded or large, to see it from this distance. Julian figured it to be a good four or five miles off, though it was hard to tell in the darkness.

In front of him, Raedrick took a step forward to follow Loran, but he stopped when Julian grabbed his arm. He looked back at Julian with questioning eyes. Julian nodded toward the distant fire. Raedrick turned his head to follow Julian's gaze, and frowned.

"Our destination," Raedrick said, certainty in his tone.

Julian nodded, swallowing despite the fact that his mouth had gone dry. He loosened his sword in its scabbard, for all the good it would do against a being like the Out-Dweller.

Raedrick gave a slow roll of his shoulders, and winced. His injured shoulder must still be paining him, and no wonder. "Well," he said, "let's get to it."

Then he followed Loran down the hill.

Julian glanced at Melanie, who still stood at his side. She wore a grim, determined expression. Their eyes met for a long moment, then she nodded at him, and her lips curled upward ever so slightly. He returned the nod.

Then, together, he and Melanie followed the others toward their destiny.

❧ 28 ❧

THE LAIR OF THE BEAST

At first glance, the camp, or base, or whatever, was nothing to look at. A lean-to lay propped up against a little spur of sheer rock that rose from the side of the hill, really the side of the mountain, as close they must have been to the true peaks of the Saddleback Range now, all twining branches with loose piles of fallen pine needles thrown atop it. It would barely keep a stiff breeze off its inhabitant, let alone a good rainfall or snowfall.

Not far from the lean-to, a bonfire burned. The same fire Julian saw from the hilltop an hour ago, though it was even larger than he would have thought, from so far away. The fire's creator had thought ahead, though. A circle of large rocks, almost knee-high, surrounded the fire, preventing it from growing beyond its intended girth.

Aside from that, there was not much else to the site. Just a makeshift wooden rack, from which dangled a couple small game animals, and a similarly rough stool that rested halfway between the fire and the lean-to.

But first glances were deceiving. All the more so in this site.

Off to the right, from Julian's perspective, and easy to miss in the immediate glare of the bonfire, the sloping ground leveled out into a flat area about the size of the front half of The Oarlock's taproom. A circle of candles, their flames flickering in the night breeze, ringed the area.

And moving around the circle, more like dancing around it, was, Julian presumed, the fugitive mage.

Julian and his companions crouched in a copse of trees, one of the final easternmost outgrowths of the Glamorwood, he presumed, about a hundred feet to the left and downhill from the camp. Summoning area. Whatever Loran wanted to call it. From that distance, it was easy to miss the comparatively dim glow of the candles, and it took Julian two tries to see the circle and its attendant after Loran pointed it out.

Julian pursed his lips as he studied the site. It was remarkably unfortified. They would be able to simply march straight up there, and nothing would stop them. Except...

"Where is the Out-Dweller?" Raedrick asked, from his position off to Julian's right.

Loran crouched between them. He shrugged, but it was difficult to see his facial expression in the dim light; they had doused his floating sphere of light once they came within a half mile of the camp. His voice was level, apparently unconcerned as he replied. "I can still feel the power of its summoning. It is out there. Somewhere."

Melanie sniffed softly. Julian glanced to his left, toward her, and smirked in agreement, though he was all but certain she could not see it.

Raedrick breathed a soft curse. "It won't let us just walk up there and disrupt the spell." He paused for a second, then added, "Will it?"

Again Loran shrugged. "We dealt it no small amount of injury. It may prefer to retreat home where it can heal easily, then deal with us later."

The way he said "deal with us" sent a shiver - no, two shivers - down Julian's spine. Bad enough they might die tonight, but even if they lived, if the Out-Dweller escaped to its own plane, it would certainly seek vengeance against them. And it had the patience of an eternal lifespan to wait to achieve it.

Wonderful. Even if they won, there was a greater than zero chance that they would, in fact, lose.

"What's the plan?" Julian asked.

There was a long second or two of silence before Loran replied. "If at all possible, I need to bring the fugitive back with me alive."

"So, what, we just walk up there and extend him an invitation?" Julian could not have concealed his incredulity with that plan if he had wanted to.

Loran turned his head toward Julian, and he...nodded. "That's it exactly, Constable," he said.

And then Loran stood up from his crouch and set off, boldly and directly, toward the campsite.

"Aw hell," Julian muttered to himself.

Julian thought sure the Out-Dweller would pounce on them as they crossed the distance between their rally point in the copse and the campsite. But for whatever reason, it did not.

It was almost as though they were taking a nighttime stroll through pristine country, so easily did they reach the limit of the bonfire's light.

Julian thought to stop at the edge of that circle, to check the lay of the land before proceeding onward. But, as always, Loran had other ideas. He strode forward with that same bold, confident gait he always seemed to use, passing into the bonfire's circle of illumination apparently without care and veering directly toward the little candle circle, and the fugitive mage.

"Telurian!" Loran bellowed as he approached the circle.

The fugitive froze in mid-step, turning eyes that glinted feral in the firelight toward Loran as the Inquisitor approached him.

Loran's steps did not slow, though Julian saw him flex his hands on his staff as Telurian's gaze settled on him.

"I am here," Loran said, somberly.

Julian followed a few steps behind Loran, Raedrick and Melanie at his side, all the while wondering if perhaps coming along was not the greatest idea in the world. And then he got a better look at Telurian.

The outlaw mage, seen up close, was pathetic. His clothing consisted of little more than tattered rags that might have been finery, a long, long time ago. His beard was scraggly, his light brown hair long and unkempt, with wisps sticking out every which way. He had to be younger than Loran, but his face was covered with so much soot and grime it was impossible to tell for sure.

But his eyes.

They were sharp, intelligent, lucid. And wild. They darted to and fro, as though he were afraid to leave his attention in any one spot for too long.

He looked haunted. Hunted.

"Master?" he croaked out, his voice raspy as though he had been shouting for a long while, or he was desperately dehydrated. In spite of that, he sounded almost relieved. Not what Julian would have expected from a fugitive.

Loran nodded, coming to a halt a half-dozen paces from Telurian.

The fugitive's eyes widened slightly, then he half laughed, half snarled. "You're too late," he said, the momentary relief leaving his voice completely. "It is done."

Julian glanced over at Melanie, hoping she had an inkling of what he meant, but she looked as confused as Julian felt. What is done?

"Nevertheless, I am here to bring you back. And you will come with me, Telurian, whether I must force you or no." Loran leaned forward, planting his staff on the ground firmly. "We both know I can do that."

Telurian shook his head, his eyes resuming their furtive dance around the area. "I cannot!" he said, sounding suddenly desperate.

"Send the beast back where it came from. Now."

Telurian recoiled beneath the power of Loran's command. It cut through the air like a whip, and for a moment the fugitive seemed stunned into stillness. Then he shook his head again and groaned. It was a sound of utmost despair, of someone who had witnessed horrors beyond belief and could not escape their memory.

"You don't understand," Telurian all but whispered, though his words carried through the air plainly. "I cannot control it."

He lowered his head, breaking contact with Loran's eyes.

At that exact moment, the earth just past the far side of the circle of candles burst open, and blackness incarnate swept over them all.

✤ 29 ✤

DANCING IN THE DARK

Julian should not have been surprised. He had been more than halfway expecting the Out-Dweller to attack them for most of the last hour or more. But regardless, when darkness flowed out of the ripped-open earth like a rolling wave, he stood rooted to the spot in shock.

And then the wave hit him, and he went reeling.

All light vanished.

All around, he heard his friends shouting, but they sounded a million miles away and he could not make out what they were saying.

Other sounds issued through the blackness, skittering sounds, like many-legged creatures crawling over stone, and he cringed.

There were...things...in the darkness, all around.

Julian drew his sword and turned a complete circle - or at least he thought it was a complete circle, but how to tell? - while listening carefully.

They were everywhere.

Off to his left, Loran's voice rose in a powerful chant that ended abruptly in a vicious-sounding word that Julian did not understand but sounded like something a judge might say to the executioner to order him to do the deed. A heartbeat later, a wave of heat swept over Julian, and he found himself driven back a couple steps.

His boot struck something momentarily, but then the thing was gone.

Uh-oh.

Julian slid away and cut downward with his sword toward whatever he had inadvertently kicked. The blade whistled through the air, meeting no resistance until the tip struck the ground in front of him. Nothing there.

Until there was.

Something struck the back of his left knee, and his leg buckled. He fell sideways, only months and months of training, honed by the stress of more battles than he wanted to remember, stopping him from landing, helpless, on his side. Instead, he tucked his shoulder and rolled, casting his sword aside as he went lest he skewer himself in the process.

A moment later, Julian was back on his feet, still just as blind as before and now feeling naked as well without nigh on three feet of sharpened steel to put between himself and...whatever that was. He settled for a little bit less than a foot, drawing his dagger from its sheath at the small of his back.

It did not offer much comfort.

The skittering noise came again, from the right this time, he thought. Julian turned to face it, part of him wondering what the point of that was, considering the thing could just move the other way to get behind him. He forced that part of him to shut up, best he could. It mostly worked.

A guttural roar, loud and full of fury—and pain?—assaulted Julian's ears. Again he stumbled a pace or so, and again his boot struck something. But this time it did not disappear as soon as he made contact. Suddenly Julian realized that the air behind him was hot. Very hot. The kind of hot that threatened to scorch him where he stood if he did not move.

The bonfire.

The skittering noise sounded again, more steadily this time, from in front of him and to his right.

It was growing louder; the thing was drawing near.

Then there was a hissing sound, almost like a man drawing a breath through a gap in teeth, and the skittering came again, more rapidly, then vanished.

The slightest gust of air against his face warned Julian of the danger, and he managed to drop to one knee before the thing, whatever it was, could hit him square in the chest. As it was, it struck the top of his left shoulder and stuck there. He almost reeled backward, into the flames, but he managed to brace himself. His nearly shouted grunt accompanied the movement of his muscles as he leaned forward, into the blow, then spun with it to the left instead of straight backwards, which undoubtedly had been the thing's plan.

Julian's left hand clamped down on the thing, whatever it was, and felt only a hard carapace, like on an beetle except so much larger it almost did not bear comparing the two. For a second, he paused, wondering about the creature that seemed to be embracing him.

And then the pain began.

When the dark wave rushed over her and she heard the skittering sounds in the darkness, Melanie had to fight back a surge of panic. Intellectually, she knew—or thought she knew—what was happening. The Out-Dweller had somehow summoned a few of its minions to this plane, to fight its battles for it. Its minions, at least the ones without the strength to resist its call—and it would not be a particularly strong call, coming from here and having to use Telurian's circle instead of one of its own—would be comparatively weak, and easy to dispatch.

Somehow, that knowledge was little comfort, there in the blackness.

She could not even see the flames that she knew flickered around her hands, the dark was so absolute. It was not just the absence of light; it was a dark the devoured any hint of radiance, a vacuum that removed all hope and joy.

They had brought a portion of their home into the material world with them.

Another skittering noise sounded, nearer than before, and the panic that had been threatening her psyche burst forth. It filled her, sending her heartbeat into a sprint so that for a few moments all she could hear was that pounding and, above it, the frantic sounds of her own breath.

They were doomed, here. She was doomed.

It was all she could do not to fall to her knees and weep in despair.

And then a voice, strong and assured, mighty, broke through the void and shattered the despair within her. She recognized the language it chanted in from Timon's earliest lessons, and for a moment she thought it was he, come back to save her.

The voice's timbre registered more fully and she recognized it. Her enemy.

Then a wave of heat struck her. And more than heat, light. A swift ribbon of flame washed over and past her, making her cringe backwards with the expectation that she had been badly burned. But when she looked down, her dress was intact and her exposed skin was untouched.

How?

She blinked, and it suddenly registered that she could see. She looked up and saw that she stood on the outer edge of a circle of light, not bright by any means but enough to see by, surrounded on all sides by blackness deeper than the darkest night. She could not tell the source of the light; it seemed to permeate the air itself within the circle. But the ring of darkness around her seemed to pulse against the light, surging inward all around as though probing for a way forward so that it could engulf her again. But it was repelled; the light prevailed, and she stood free to move and see the world around her.

But not alone.

Across the circle from her, Loran nodded with a certain satisfaction and glanced about. When his gaze fell on her, his lips turned upwards into something that almost, but not quite, more resembled a grin than a condescending sneer.

"I wondered whether you would be able to make it through," he said. "It seems you are not insignificant, after all."

Melanie just stared at him, confusion stealing her retort from her.

Loran read her lack of understanding from her expression and sneered all the deeper. "Or maybe not. Did your man Timon teach you nothing of this?"

She glanced around at the little space of light. It was still just her and Loran. She tried to put on an apathetic, or at least knowing, expression as she shrugged.

Mocking laughter was his only response at first. Finally, after several seconds, he brought himself under control and actually smiled at her. "The outside minions do not just bring darkness; they bring the essence of their plane itself. For as long as the summoning circle stands, this area is now, for all intents and purposes, part of their world, not ours."

Melanie swallowed. Hard. "So, you..."

"I brought forward a small area of our reality into their plane."

His words struck her like a sledgehammer. What he was describing... "That's not possible," she breathed. "A rift takes..."

Loran snorted with such derision she almost melted. "Did I say I created a rift, woman?" He looked at her incredulously and shook his head. Then he turned his back on her and raised his hands over his head, his staff held between them, parallel to the ground. He drew a deep breath and held it for a few seconds. When he let it out, he spoke again, and his tone was completely calm, completely cool and focused. "I have re-imposed our world onto the artificiality that these beings forced on it. There is no need for a rift; it is they who caused the disruption of our plane, not vice versa." He glanced back at her and crooked an eyebrow upwards. "The Out-Dweller will sense that imposition, and take it as a challenge. Any moment now."

Just then, right on cue, a guttural roar, so loud it felt as though it must overwhelm her and knock her senseless, issued forth from the surging blackness in front of Melanie and Loran. Then the roar ended, as quickly as it began.

Silence reigned for a few seconds, and even the dark ring seemed to grow still around them.

And then the darkness swelled upward and inward, toward them. The light in their little circle seemed to dim, and for a second Melanie thought it would go out altogether. And all at once, she understood why it just might.

The Out-Dweller approached.

❧ 30 ❧

HARD PRESSED

Melanie swallowed hard, trying to press down the sudden terror that surged within her. It was one thing to cast spells at the Out-Dweller from afar. But now it was coming, and only she and Loran stood before it.

She wiped a sudden sweat from her brow and was not surprised that her hand trembled as she did so. She hated to admit it, but the presence of Julian and Raedrick, and the steel of their blades, useless as it was against this foe, had offered her some comfort. Now, without them...

The darkness bulged inward like a blister, and right then a scream echoed from somewhere to Melanie's right. A man's scream, full of pain and fear. It only took a second for her to recognize Julian's voice.

The fear swelled within her, but so also did anger. Her dear friend was being tortured by this beast, or its minions.

It would pay.

"What should I do?" She hated to ask Loran for advice, but he was right. Timon had taught her next to nothing about dealing with the Out-Dwellers, just that they existed and the very basics of how a summoning worked. She could never achieve a summoning herself, and she was not foolish enough to try; if by some chance she gained the attention of one able to use a call as meager as hers to bring itself over...

Well, she had this night seen what such a creature would be like. She shuddered to think of trying to control it by herself.

Loran grunted, his eyes now fixed on the bulging blister of blackness. Any second now, the Out-Dweller would emerge, and he stood straight and tall to meet it. "I can banish it. Here." He paused, then added, "But I may need your help to hold it."

He said no more, and he would not see the gesture, but Melanie nodded. Hold it in place. She could do that.

She hoped.

"It comes." Loran could have been commenting on the return of a dog sent to fetch a downed pheasant, as much inflection as he put into his voice.

For Melanie's part, as the blister finally popped, it was all she could do not to retreat. Not that it made any great noise, or sent any force her way. But it concealed a thing of darkness, of powerful evil, and it would...

A figure fell to the earth as the blister of blackness burst and retreated back to the edge of their circle of light. Not particularly tall, though taller than Loran - who wasn't? - and thin, it was a man. He lay on his belly with his face in the dirt, but she knew immediately who he was.

Telurian.

Melanie blinked in surprise. "Is that supposed to..."

Loran shook his head. "No." He lowered his staff and frowned, then glanced back at her again. "No, that was supposed to be the Out-Dweller." He strode slowly forward, to Telurian's side, and squatted down. Pressing his fingers to the side of the fallen mage's throat, Loran paused for a few seconds, then nodded quickly. "He lives."

"Great." Melanie turned a quick circle, looking all around. It still was only she and Loran. "Now what?"

A second male voice cried out in pain from somewhere out in the blackness. Raedrick. Only then did Melanie to notice that

Julian had ceased his cries. Gods, let him be alright. She was surprised to find how her heart ached over the notion that he may not be.

Not that she was any more worried about him than Raedrick. Of course not.

"Now," Loran said, returning to his full height and scowling out at the blackness that encircled them. He paused, then took a breath and continued. "Now, I begin a banishment ritual."

Melanie blinked in confusion. "Doesn't the Out-Dweller need to be present for that?"

Loran's scowl became a condescending sneer as he looked at her. "It *is* present, woman. This will take longer, and be more diffi-cult, than if it were close enough for physical contact. But if it is within the boundaries of the summoning area, it cannot resist being expelled from our world, if the ritual is done correctly."

With that, he lowered his staff and turned a full circle, tracing a line in the dirt at his feet as he dragged the staff over the ground in time with his turn. His eyes met Melanie's, and she saw scorn - what else could she expect from the likes of him - but also resolve. But beneath that, fear.

Loran was afraid.

That made sense. Melanie was nearly beside herself with fear; she had never imagined a creature such as this Out-Dweller. It went well beyond the most stern warnings Timon had given her against trying her had at summoning, and those warnings had been energetic indeed. And she had taken them to heart; she certainly never thought to actually face a being such as this.

But Loran had been trained in summoning. As an Inquisitor of the Magestirium, he was intimately familiar with every school of magic, every incantation and ritual. If *he* was scared...

Melanie felt her bowels go to water, and it was all she could do not to flee right then and there. Of course, where would she run to? The darkness waited on all sides; there could be no escape for her, not without victory. So she gritted her teeth and inhaled deeply through her nose, then exhaled out of her mouth, keeping up a slow and steady rhythm despite her body screaming at her that she needed to pant, to get more air into her lungs more quickly NOW!

After a minute or so of forcibly slow, controlled breathing, she felt the panic fade. Only healthy fear remained, the kind of fear that could be acknowledged and controlled, but would not rule her.

Again her eyes met Loran's, and he gave her the slightest of nods.

Then he set to chanting.

RITUAL SACRIFICE

The words Loran used were in a tongue Melanie had never heard before. They were guttural, brutal, and harsh, the kinds of words that could never be sung but only screamed in fury. But Loran spoke them smoothly, in a perfectly controlled tone of voice that never raised or lowered, but continued as though he were speaking to a friend in a quiet sitting room.

But in spite of that, Loran's words cut through the dark of the night, and the deeper, unnatural blackness of the Out-Dweller and its minions, with apparent ease. His voice echoed around the area, and with each syllable, it seemed the blackness around he and Melanie retreated a bit.

He was doing it!

Hope slowly grew in Melanie's breast as the ring of blackness moved slowly but steadily away from them, and the circle of light in which she stood grew in time with the blackness' retreat. If that darkness truly consisted of elements from the Out-Dweller's home plane, and not of the mere absence of light in this world, its retreat could only mean that the Out-Dweller, mighty as it obviously was, could indeed be beaten.

The circle expanded a bit more, the darkness retreating at a more rapid pace. Melanie looked around, and saw the same thing occurring all around the circle. Until she saw the spot directly behind Loran.

There, the darkness, instead of retreating, pulled in on itself. It seemed to roil and swirl, like clouds during a thunderstorm. The circle of light pushed outward again, but there in that one place the blackness held firm, a bulging pustule of evil that held out against the light's advance.

Melanie fell back a half-step, swallowing hard. Hope, which had so suddenly surged within her, faded, turning to fear as that pustule of blackness pulsed, then swelled upward and outward, toward her.

Then the pustule burst.

Whipping tendrils of blackness shot forth, the same things the Out-Dweller had used against them before, and Melanie had no doubt the beast stood within that swirling blackness.

She heard herself crying out, chanting a quick incantation before she even realized she was doing it. Again fire blazed around her hands, and she sent out twin lances of flame to meet the advancing tendrils. The two forces met; fire against living blackness, and for a second Melanie thought she might be able to hold them back completely. But the blackness whipped and writhed, impossibly flexible. After the first resistance from her flames, they retreated, but then simply twisted around her spell, moving to her and Loran's flanks.

Then a third and a forth tendril joined the first two.

"Loran!" Melanie cried out in alarm.

But he paid no heed. He was deep into his incantation, his face a mask of concentration. Even if he had heard her through his focus, he could do nothing to help her. Locked into the banishing ritual as he was, he could not stop. To do so would be to invite disaster when the energy he had built up within the incantation sought release, in whatever random manner it could.

Melanie was on her own.

The tendrils, all four of them, squirmed closer. They lowered their speed for a moment, as though testing the area for threats, before proceeding onward. Her flames had taught them caution, at the least.

Part of her shouted with glee at that. Seldom had she had the opportunity to face off against another person, or being, who was magical in nature. Back when the opportunities were plentiful - and there never had been that many - she had given as good as she got more often than not. So Melanie knew she was no slouch. But it was one thing to face off against a fellow novice in the art and prevail, or at least break even. It was something else for a being as powerful as the Out-Dweller, from a plane as evil as the sun was hot, to recoil from her attacks.

This was the second time her fire had injured, or at the very least frightened, the beast.

But then, as the black tendrils began to pick up speed as the came for her—and Loran, though part of her scoffed that she did not care in the least if he were taken except that it would prevent her own revenge—the momentary injury she had apparently given the Out-Dweller at the sisters' house, and again out in the grass, mattered very little.

Fire was not the right tool to use. It had given the tendrils pause, but only momentarily. She needed something else.

Melanie sought through her mind, considering the various spells Timon had taught her and discarding them, one by one, as useless in this situation.

The tendrils swept closer, and she felt beads of sweat running down her brow, the growing panic within her threatening to break through.

There had to be something!

She glanced back at Loran again, but he was still wrapped up in his ritual chanting. How much longer would it take?

The first of the tendrils suddenly whipped forward at a speed she had never seen before. In an instant, cold so intense it burned wrapped around her legs just above the ankle and a force too strong to resist tugged her toward the pustule of darkness.

She fell, her back striking the earth unceremoniously. Caught up in the tendril as her legs were, she could not roll with the fall or do much of anything to reduce its force, and she lost her breath as the wind was knocked out of her.

She had to breathe!

But the air would not come. For several terrifying seconds, the only thing that registered in Melanie's mind was the lack of air, and she thought perhaps a tendril had wrapped around her body, constricting like a snake.

Then, at last, she managed to inhale, and it was like iced water on a sweltering day. She wanted nothing more than to lie there and exalt in the sheer joy of breathing, where just a moment ago she thought she might never do so again.

Then the force about her legs tugged again and she began to drag across the ground toward the bulging blackness, where the Out-Dweller waited. The relief that flooded through her with that first breath fled as quickly as it came and she had to hold back a whimper of despair.

It was so strong! She clawed at the ground, trying to arrest her motion, to no avail. If anything, her movement became more rapid.

She tried to kick her legs, to pull them free of the tendril, but they would not move. The thing was strong, but it was more than that. That burning cold, forgotten in her loss of breath, crept slowly up from where the thing was wrapped around her calves and had now reached her thighs. Where it passed was only numb, like her legs no longer existed; she was certain she could not have moved her legs below the knees even if the thing had let her go.

Fear surged higher, becoming almost panic.

She could not give in to it. That way led only to death.

Melanie looked back at the tendril and only then realized it was just that: a single tendril. But there had been four. Where were...

Loran!

She craned her neck, twisting as best she could to see him. Had he been taken as well?

Then he came into view, and the scene around the Inquisitor stopped her cold.

He stood there, looking for all the world as though nothing untoward was happening as he continued his ritual chant. As far as she could tell, he had not even looked up. The three tendrils of blackness hovered in the air all around him. They quivered with pent up energy as though eager to attack but hesitant, unsure as to what he was doing.

Melanie could relate. He was not a fool. Why would he leave himself so wide open?

All three tendrils struck at the same time, darting toward the mage at lightning speed. He could not hope to repel them all, not as quickly as they were moving.

He did not have to.

When the tendrils reached a distance of about three feet from Loran, they stopped completely. A glowing blue nimbus erupted where each stopped, bright like a campfire in the immediate vicinity of each tendril but growing quickly less luminous as the glow spread away from it. The light spread around, the three sources reinforcing each other enough to show the outline of a dome completely surrounding Loran, who still stood, chanting, apparently completely unconcerned about the attack his magic had just prevented.

That bastard!

He had set a defensive barrier up around himself, but spared not a thought for Melanie, not even to inform her of that fact. And why not? She was just an abomination in his eyes, a beast to be put down. A beast he had to tolerate, for the moment, but if she were to fall in battle with the Out-Dweller, that would solve one of his problems for him, wouldn't it. Raedrick and Julian could not possibly fault him for her death in these circumstances.

She clenched her teeth, burning anger eclipsing her near-panic in a heartbeat. No, she would not give him that satisfaction.

The tendril about her calves yanked again, and Melanie was shocked to see she was almost to the barrier of blackness. Less than ten feet now, and that fiery cold now reached up to her hips.

It would drag her into the darkness in another few seconds. And once that happened...there would be no hope out there, beyond the light.

Down at the deepest register of her hearing, so low it came across as a vibration in her body as much as a sound impacting her ears, a rumble sounded. It only lasted for a second, but it twisted upward in pitch at the very end, making it sound almost sardonic.

Melanie realized what it was. The Out-Dweller's laughter.

And then the tendril pulled at her legs again, and the blackness swelled up to receive her.

❧ 32 ❧

THE WAITING BLACKNESS

There was no more time to think. There was barely time to react at all. As the blackness loomed closer, towering overhead like a wave about to crash down all around her, Melanie dipped her hand into the pouch that kept her spell components.

Her fingers quickly traced the shape of a carefully wrapped item and clenched around it, reacting to its familiar feel with the instinctive insight of hundreds of caresses, hundreds of incantations. She knew this thing without needing to think on it: the essence of the very first spell Timon had ever taught her.

The words of the incantation swept off her tongue without effort, so often had she given them voice in the past. Even had she the time to pull out her spell book, she would not have needed to consult it, so intimate was the spell. As she chanted and brought her hands together, crushing the cloth-wrapped seeds between them and twisting, she saw Timon's face, his dark green eyes sparkling with pride the way they had the first time she had successfully done this.

And then light, pure white light, erupted from her hands where the component was consumed, and spread outward.

She had put more into the illumination spell than she realized.

It had never burned this brightly before. It out-shown a dozen lanterns, but somehow it was not painful to look at.

At least not for her.

The Out-Dweller, on the other hand...

It let out a shriek, from surprise as much as from pain, Melanie thought. But suddenly the tendril's grip on her legs eased and it seemed as though the blackness, which had been about to consume her a mere second before, was again drawing back, as it had from Loran's earlier spell. Except that this time it was like a rapid retreat more than a grudging withdrawal.

Understanding came all at once, and Melanie cursed herself, silently, for a fool. The Out-Dweller dwelt in a world of darkness. Here on this plane, it had surrounded itself in darkness. In some ways, maybe it *was* darkness. Loran's attack, back at the sisters' house, had been one of light. Melanie's fire had been the deciding factor in driving it off. Maybe. But how much of that was because of the fire's heat and how much because of the light that came with it?

Melanie was beginning to think more of the latter than the former.

She shouted a secondary incantation and pushed upward with her hands, and the blazing light raised a few feet up into the air, then sat there, shining away. It would not last long, but maybe long enough.

She pulled another packet of seeds from her pouch and began the primary incantation again.

Almost immediately the tendril eased its grip further, as though anticipating the illumination to come. When it did come, the tendril shot backwards, away from her as it released its grip entirely.

With satisfaction, Melanie spat a curse at the thing. The satisfaction faded when she realized she still could not move her legs. Scowling, she again floated the ball of light then used her palms to push herself back away from the barrier of blackness as quickly as she could.

When she had put ten feet from herself and the Out-Dweller—somehow she knew it still lurked there, ahead of her—she pushed herself up to a seated position and again chanted the incantation of light. Again she crushed the seeds, and again her little glowing ball appeared.

Then she spoke the incantation again, and again the component was destroyed.

The ball of light grew larger, and far, far brighter.

Again. And again.

And then she placed her hand into her pouch and found no more of the carefully-wrapped seeds.

It would have to do. And it looked like it was beginning to. All around, the blackness was pushing away from their circle again, and even the tendrils that were still attacking Loran pulled back, their aggression fading before the onslaught of illumination from Melanie's spell. She dared think that this one spell, multiplied onto itself as many times as it had been, might be enough to protect them completely for as long as Loran needed to finish the ritual.

Except that this time she did not intend to merely float it in place.

She drew her hand back, and the ball went with it. As she brought her hand forward again, she shouted out the secondary incantation, with a little added twist at the end, and the ball of brightness flew from her fingers. It flashed between its little siblings, hanging there in the air nonchalantly, and impacted the barrier of blackness.

It was like a stone dropping into a still pool of water.

The blackness boiled backward from the ball of light, flooding away from it in a wave that sped in both directions around the circle. Then the ball of light sunk deeper, and the blackness closed in behind it and it was gone.

Melanie blinked, drawing in a quick breath as the momentary elation she had felt over the spell's apparent success faded a bit.

Like the dirt kicked up by the stone impacting the bottom of the pool, light flared through the blackness in a hundred different places. Pinpricks and gaping beams of radiance swelled from the darkness, their number spreading outward from where the ball struck like a rash, but a rash of purity.

And then, with a brilliant flash, the darkness was ripped asunder. Little bits of blackness flew in all directions like dust before a great wind. Even as they flew, the bits of black seemed to shrivel and crumple apart until they disappeared entirely.

Melanie sat there, stunned at what had just happened. It took her a moment to take it all in, and to fully comprehend what she was now seeing.

Off to her right, a group of black, shiny....things...writhed around atop each other in a little pile. They scrambled as though fighting over something. A second pile lay off to the left, this one larger, made up of more of the beasts. Whatever they were, their sudden illumination made both piles stop their ceaseless motion. Then, a second later, the things began retreating, scampering back from the new light, toward the shadows of the tree line and between rocks on the mountain's flank. In ones and twos at first, then it greater numbers, and with greater speed, they went.

Melanie only noticed them in passing though. The Out-Dweller held all of her attention.

It had fallen onto its back, but it was slowly regaining its feet. In the replenished firelight and the illumination of her two floating lights, the beast was fully revealed; the smokey shadows that had obscured it before were gone, cast asunder by the force of the light she had used.

It was massive, more powerfully built than she had realized, and it had seemed barrel-chested enough before. Rippling muscles beneath scaly flesh that housed spikes and thorns of all sizes promised no end of pain when it took her. And the fire smoldering in its double-pair of eyes promised that no matter how she fought, how she resisted, it would take her, and bring her back to its home plane with it when it finally departed her world. And never grant her the release of death.

The promise of eternal punishment for her insolence bore down on her mind, the certainty of the Out-Dweller's victory casting all hope aside. She wanted to scream, to push herself away. To find a way, any way, to escape. To hide. To pull a mountain down atop herself, if only it would protect her from this beast's wrath. But she could not bring herself to look away from its fiery stare, and the agony it promised.

The Out-Dweller smiled, or made an expression that could she could only understand as a smile, hot in its gleeful malevolence, and took a step toward her. Then another.

Melanie's mind screamed to run, but her legs were still numb to the hip and did not respond. Or maybe she did not want them to respond. Suddenly she could not remember why she should.

Those eyes. They seemed to grow larger, opening wide to engulf her. Large as the Out-Dweller was, they made the rest of it seem tiny by comparison. She saw through them and gasped. Within lay fire, beautiful and terrible fire, that promise to caress even as it rent her soul asunder.

She shuddered. She screamed. She moaned.

But she could not move.

It was directly atop her now, the sickly sweet-sour stench of its body filling her nose, making her want to gag as the taste of it seemed to penetrate her tongue as well. It reached down with its huge talons, digits that would tear her flesh apart at the lightest grip. And still she sat still, fascinated by the play of fire within its eyes. It was so brilliant, so agonizing, so seductive.

A sudden new noise reached her ears. Coming from behind her somewhere, it seemed extremely loud, but for some reason she could barely register it. The noise was not worthy of her notice, not compared with the nearly-audible roar of the inferno within those eyes.

The Out-Dweller, though...

The noise seemed to strike it like a physical blow. The beast stopped midway toward grabbing her and fell back a half-step. Its head quirked upward, breaking contact with Melanie's gaze to stare at something behind her.

Reality came back to her in a rush. What had been happening in Lydelton these last several nights. The journey through the grass to this site. The battle against the darkness. Reality. And with it, all-consuming horror over what had almost just happened.

She did scream then, and fell backward onto the dirt, throwing up her hands defensively as though that alone could ward off the gargantuan beast that stood less than one of its paces away from her.

Again that new noise came, intruding on Melanie's sudden panic as she recognized it for what it was: Loran's voice.

He had spoken a single word, using the same guttural tongue he had been chanting in at the start of the ritual. That word must have held some measure of power, because again the Out-Dweller moved backwards.

Though not as far this time. It steeled itself visibly and managed to shrug off most of the effect of Loran's spell, whatever it was.

One of its great talon-hands moved behind its back, and when it emerged again, the talons were clasped around something long, black, and serpentine. Melanie cringed even more than she was already as she recognized it for what it was: a great whip. But not like any whip she had ever seen. This one cast about even though the Out-Dweller held its handle motionless.

Then it flicked in her direction and she scrambled backwards. It missed her, barely, but she got a better look at it as it did, and she screamed again at this latest horror.

The whip was alive. A living serpent, black and hooded around its head, like a cobra. Its eyes burned red like the Out-Dweller's, as did its fangs. Drops of some foul fluid dripped from its mouth, sizzling the earth where they fell at Melanie's side.

She kicked herself backwards again, but then stopped, surprised. Her legs worked!

A moment ago, they had been colder than deepest winter and completely immobile. Now, they at least obeyed her commands, even though they did not feel all that much warmer.

How...?

But there was no time the wonder about that right then. Loran shouted again, but this time the Out-Dweller did not move backward. Instead, it flicked the serpent-whip in his direction. It seemed to lengthen as it moved, stretching further than Melanie would have thought possible, and then even more; it would have no trouble crossing the distance between the Out-Dweller and the Inquisitor.

He could not possibly avoid the whip, as quickly as it came toward him, but he seemed unconcerned. He still had his shield, after all...

The serpent-whip struck Loran's shield, and again the blue-light flashed around him. Then the whip continued onward toward him.

Loran's eyes widened in surprise. In sudden fear. And then the serpent-whip struck him and he vanished beneath the serpent's coils.

❧ 33 ❧

ENFLAMED

Melanie cried out in denial as Loran was engulfed. It could not take him!

Let it.

The thought came unbidden, and with it a wave of self-loathing. What cared she if the Inquisitor was killed here this night? She had been ready to do it herself not so long ago. Only her realization that she - that they - needed Loran for this night's work, and her friends' intervention, had stopped her. He had been more than eager to profit from her death this night as well. What was good for the goose was good for the gander.

Hell, she ought to dance a jig and thank the Out-Dweller for saving her the trouble.

And you can take that thing yourself, can you?

She looked away from the squirming serpent coils, all that was visible where the Inquisitor was a moment ago, and toward the Out-Dweller. It wore a cruelly satisfied expression, or at least that is how Melanie interpreted the look on its face, as its whip did its work.

She swallowed and pushed herself to her feet. She wobbled for several heartbeats, but managed to retreat a step, both grateful that she was no longer the focus of the Out-Dweller's attention and ashamed by the truth she knew without a doubt.

Without Loran she could not prevail, and she would die here tonight. Or maybe not. The promise of being dragged to the beast's plane and tormented for its pleasure, forever, returned to its place at the front of her brain.

Melanie snarled, in anger at the horror that promise evoked within her and at the helplessness she had felt just moments ago, beneath the beast's gaze. And in frustration that she was going to have to come to Loran's aid. Again. It just was not fair. But there was no help for it.

She considered, and rejected, a number of components from within her pouch. All were for spells that she knew would be useless in this fight.

Light. She needed more light.

But she could not find any. No components for any illumination spell she knew remained within her pouch, and without them...

Her fingers closed on something soft, almost crumbly. Withdrawing the carefully-wrapped object from the pouch, she brought it up to her nose and inhaled. She knew the sulfurous odor would be nearly enough to overpower her, knew what this material was for, but all the same she had to confirm it.

It had been months, more months than she wanted to think, since she had attempted this spell. It had been among the last Timon taught her, though truth be told she never had truly gotten the hang of it. She had forgotten she still had this component mixture at all; she must have grabbed it up by accident while she was packing her equipment for the night.

Fortunate that she had. If she could pull this spell off...

Loran cried out, more a shout of power and command than anything else, and for a moment the coiling snake-whip expanded as though being repulsed by some tremendous force. But then, just as quickly, the coils collapsed back down. Loran's next cry was one of anger and...fear? He did not have much time left, if he was letting that show.

Trying not to remind herself that she was about to save his sorry neck for the second time in one night, Melanie clapped her hands together, bursting the sulfur mixture's casing and smearing the concoction all over her palms. Then she turned so she could see the bonfire from the corner of her eye and raised her arms, one pointing at the bonfire and the other at the Out-Dweller.

Then she began her incantation

The pain lasted for an eternity, and just when it seemed it would never end, it got worse. It spread from his chest and shoulder to his arm to his belly to his leg to his other arm to both hands to his feet, and on and on until there was not a single part of his body that did not burn with agony. Any one of the points of pain would have been bearable. Any two or three, maybe. But dozens...

He vaguely recalled screaming, screaming until he had no more breath to scream with, despite the urge to scream all the more, all the louder. But it was all he could do to gasp in a what should have been a lung-full of air. But instead, all that came through was the barest of breezes, not nearly enough to satisfy his need. He tried again, somehow, but again it was not enough. Not enough to allow him to scream, and also not enough to quench his need for fresh air, though it was just enough to stop him from passing out

This new torment, the agony of being smothered without release, built upon his other pain until his entire world consisted of nothing else.

Had there ever *been* anything else?

He did not know; he could see nothing but blackness, hear nothing but that awful skittering sound and the last remnants of his scream, smell nothing but a rancid stink like rotting meat, think of nothing except for his torment, and the desperate need to escape it. But try though he might, he could not move to get away.

And so he lay there, a tiny part of his mind managing to wonder how long this could go on before he went well and truly mad.

There was no answer.

Time, if there was such a thing as time, slowed to a crawl, each moment an eternity of torment that was only eclipsed by the next. And then the next.

And then, all at once, something changed.

His foot ceased hurting. Then his lower leg. Slowly, but with a quickening pace, his other limbs and then his torso ceased their endless ache until, all at once, the last of the agony left him.

His lungs functioned again. He breathed in the largest gulp of air he ever had and cracked his eyes open.

A new agony assaulted him as light, light so bright it threatened to blind him, forced him to turn his head away and clench his eyes shut again.

A blessedly long moment devoid of pain passed, and he tried again. This time he could see without as much difficulty; the brilliant light had dimmed.

Regardless, he could make out details. A large fire burning off to his left. Trees at the edge of the darkness beyond it. And...things...black insectoid things scurrying away from him, or more correctly away from the source of that brilliant light and toward the shadows on all sides.

Revulsion filled him as he realized that those things had been all over him, that they were what had caused all his pain. He quickly felt all over himself, but could find no wounds, or any hint of one. So how...

A loud cry from the rear caused him to turn around.

A woman stood not far away. Dark-haired and lovely, wearing a dress that had once been fine but now was an irreconcilable mess and a frightened expression on her face. And to the left, a great mammoth beast that clutched some sort of whip in one hand.

The beast brought the whip down, and it coiled around a small man, who collapsed beneath the weight of the strange whip's coils.

It all came back to him in a rush. The Out-Dweller. Loran. The murders. Melanie.

Julian grunted and forced himself to stand, but only got as far as rolling over and pushing himself to his hands and knees when Melanie drew something from her belt pouch and rubbed it between her hands. Then she said a quick incantation, in a tone of voice he remembered from her so well: the tone that said she was trying not to show how frightened she was, and that fear made her angry.

Any sane man would stay away from a woman speaking in a tone like that.

She finished the incantation and waited. For a couple seconds, nothing happened. Then the heat from the bonfire at his back doubled, no tripled at least, and the entire area was bathed in a yellow-white glow that reminded Julian of a piece of metal that had just been withdrawn from a smith's forge.

The Out-Dweller recoiled from that burst of light, lifting its free hand to shield its eyes.

A heartbeat later, a horizontal column of white flame, as thick around as both of Julian's thighs put together, struck the beast in its chest. Strangely, it did not seem as though the flame was hurting it very much; no smoke rose from its chest, despite the scorching heat of the flame. All the same, the Out-Dweller stumbled backwards, raising its other hand to cover its eyes and letting the strange whip fall to the ground.

As soon as the whip's handle struck the ground, its coils exploded outward and Loran rose from a crouch, his staff held in both hands in front of himself. He looked harried and he bled from his nose and the left side of his neck. But right then, the expression he wore was one of surprised amazement as he beheld the flame Melanie was directing against the Out-Dweller. His eyes flicked from the beast to the bonfire to Melanie, and he mouthed something soundlessly to himself.

Then, all at once, the great stream of fire winked out and the area was plunged back into comparative blackness.

Julian blinked, and for a moment could not make out anything at all while his eyes adjusted. Then, by the comparative dimness of the two floating globes of light, he saw the Out-Dweller beginning to recover itself, and his spirits sank. What happened to that fire?

He looked over his shoulder and saw that the bonfire, so large just a few minutes ago, had been reduced to little more than a softly-glowing pile of ash. A few larger coals smoldered in the center of the fire pit, but that was it. In a flash of insight, Julian realized what had happened. Melanie's spell had not created the fire, or lent it any extra power. It had merely sped up the rate it went through its fuel, consuming every scrap of it, and all the energy it contained, in a few moments, as opposed to the hours it would normally have taken to burn down.

Pretty impressive, but where did that leave them now? Right back where they started, from what Julian could tell.

The smart thing to do was run. Every fiber of his being told him to do that.

Across the way, Julian saw Raedrick stirring, pushing himself up. Melanie showed no signs of backing off, and annoyingly enough, Loran was stalking toward the Out-Dweller, his lips compressed into a determined scowl.

Muttering in annoyance about his lack of good sense, Julian boosted himself up onto his feet and grabbed up his dagger, which lay on the ground near his feet. Then, stumbling every other step and wishing again that he had his sword, he advanced.

❦ 34 ❦

THE CASTING OUT

W hy had he bothered to grab his dagger? Julian did not fool himself: there was no way that small blade, well-constructed and finely-honed as it was, could do any real harm to the Out-Dweller. The beast was not of this world, and if Loran and Melanie's magics could do little more than stun it for a moment, the thought of his sword doing any better, let alone his dagger, was just laughable.

But laughable or not, Julian led with the tip of his blade as he charged. The Out-Dweller was not focused on him; the mages—Melanie *was* a mage, no matter what those asses in the Magestirium might say—received that honor. Maybe he could get that kidney strike in, after all.

On the opposite side of the brute, Raedrick had regained his feet, though he looked decidedly dazed. His scabbard was empty, his Tyrashi blade nowhere to be seen, but just that minute it looked like Raedrick had other concerns, namely not falling back down again.

It would be a while before he would be good for it. The fight would likely be over first. Too bad; it would have been nice to make a two-flank attack.

Oh well.

Julian's foot caught in a little hollow of earth and he stumbled, pinwheeling his arms and taking a quick hopping step to prevent landing on his face. As it was, he came to a halt about a dozen paces from the Out-Dweller, suddenly off his equilibrium.

It was then that he noticed one of the Out-Dweller's glowing red eyes, staring at him.

He was not sure how he knew it was watching him; the thing did not have pupils that Julian could see. But nonetheless, the thing had regained its balance and he was certain it was watching him with one eye, and the mages with the other three. Or really, two. It probably was keeping an eye on Raedrick as well.

The bottom fell out of Julian's stomach as he thought of how confusing it would be to interpret those disparate viewpoints. But apparently the Out-Dweller had none of the difficulty a human would, and that ruled out his being able to get in a surprise attack at the beast's flank.

A sound, almost like a crack of thunder but more short-lived and deeper, emanated from the Out-Dweller. Julian could have sworn it had snorted at his attempt. In...amusement?

And then the beast drew itself up to its full height and roared, baring the multitude of triangular, razor-sharp teeth that festooned its mouth. It was more like the impact from a shield-bash than a sound. It smacked into Julian's body and sent him stumbling backwards several steps, only quick backpedalling stopping him from falling over.

Raedrick, dazed as he still was, was not so quick, and he went over onto his backside. Melanie as well.

But when the roar reached Loran, a shimmering blue dome sprang to life all around him, glowing strongly for a half-second before fading into transparency once again.

The mage sniffed and looked at the Out-Dweller with a sneer. "Enough of this," he said in a smooth, calm voice. Whatever bumps and bruises he had taken so far tonight, they did not seem to have shaken his bravado. Then he spoke a single word that

Julian did not understand and spun his staff over his head in a dizzying circular arc.

All around the flat area, candles, which had been lit when the group arrived before but had extinguished when the blackness rolled in, flickered to life, their little flames dim counterpoints to the two suspended balls of light. But somehow the candles' combined glow seemed stronger, more insistent, than those conjured balls.

The Out-Dweller blew out a hard breath through its nose - Julian had not noticed its nostrils before, two sets of vertical slits that lay between the pairs of eyes - and roared again. It was less loud this time, almost more tentative as though the beast were suddenly uncertain. Julian noticed one of its eyes tracking around toward the candles for a second.

And then it charged, straight toward Loran.

The Out-Dweller's hoofed feet tore great rivets in the ground as it rushed him, moving much faster than Julian would have thought a being of its bulk would be capable of. It closed the distance between itself and the mage in seconds and extended its arms, the great curved talons thrusting toward Loran. There was no way the mage could avoid being impaled, not as quickly as the beast had moved.

But somehow, when the Out-Dweller's talons reached him, Loran was no longer there. He vanished, reappearing six feet to his right, facing the Out-Dweller from its side.

Julian blinked in surprise, his jaw dropping open wide. What had Loran just done, and in the name of all that was holy, how?

This was no time to worry about it, however.

The Out-Dweller whirled toward Loran instantly. He was already within reach of the beast's great arms; again they lashed out toward him.

But Loran was the quicker. He spoke a hurried trio of words and thrust forward with his staff. What could only be called a hammer of light leapt from the end of his staff and struck at the beast even as it was bringing its arms down. Instead of tearing him to shreds, the Out-Dweller was lifted bodily off the ground and hurled backwards almost ten feet before it crashed to the ground on its back.

"Now, woman!" Loran barked.

Melanie had just regained her feet. She brushed her hair back from her face, clearing her vision, and cocked her head toward him, an eyebrow rising in an unspoken question.

Loran rolled his eyes disgustedly. "Hold it! Keep it on the ground!"

How in the hell was she supposed to do that?

Julian would have bet Melanie was wondering the same thing, but if she did she did not voice it. She merely nodded as though Loran had not just asked her to do the nigh-on impossible and stepped forward, one hand dipping into a pouch at her waist while the other pulled her notebook out and thumbed open a tabbed page.

Incredulity filled Julian. What was she going to do, read about it?

But he should have known better. She glanced at the page for the briefest of seconds, then began a quick, precise chant that took only slightly longer than the glance had been. The incantation culminated in her throwing a small object, the thing she had taken from her pouch Julian was sure, at the Out-Dweller, which was just beginning to get itself righted.

The object Melanie threw landed on the ground a pace away from the Out-Dweller, and for a second or two nothing happened.

The Out-Dweller got itself up onto its hands and knees and was beginning to push itself erect again. Julian's heart sank. Whatever the spell had been, it had not worked, or Melanie had missed.

Suddenly, the earth cracked open where the object Melanie threw landed. Great green shoots grew out of the crack, a half dozen of them, each twisting a different direction as it grew and each sprouting leaves as it went. The plant moved as though it were a sentient being, its shoots ensnaring the Out-Dweller in a dozen different ways between one breath and the next, and still it grew, its twining vines becoming more and more intricately inter-connected until Julian could not tell where one of the shoots stopped and the next began.

Neither, apparently, could the Out-Dweller. It howled in fury, but Julian could also detect a note of frustration there as well, as the rapidly growing plant caught it in its embrace. The beast struggled, ripping at the plant with its talons and trying to pull away using sheer strength and mass.

At first, for all its thrashings, the Out-Dweller was well and truly caught. But the plant's growth slowed and then stopped, and within moments it became clear that the Out-Dweller would be the winner in the contest between the two of them.

But it would take time.

The Out-Dweller ripped a growth of vine off, but there were literally dozens more to remove before it would be free of the plant.

It was a brilliant spell. But was it brilliant enough? Julian looked away from the Out-Dweller toward the mages.

Melanie watched the Out-Dweller struggling to free itself, her face a mask of concentration, and Julian realized she still must be controlling the plant's actions in some way.

Loran, too, was deep in conversation, but he was also chant-ing, a deep, rhythmic incantation that rolled off his tongue barely any louder than if he were having a conversation over tea. And yet, those incantations fairly boomed with power. The candles all around them pulsed in time with his words, and the breeze began to pick up.

Slowly at first, but then faster and faster, the breeze became a gust and then a full-on wind that swirled all around the flattened area. The circle of candles flickered, their flames dancing in time with the wind's movements. Julian was sure they should have gone out, extinguished by the suddenly fierce blow, but instead the flames merely moved with the wind's motion. If anything, the little flames grew, becoming torches in their own right and bathing the entire area in a radiance that came to almost rival the morning just after sunrise.

The Out-Dweller bellowed and raised its arms almost reflexively against the suddenly more intense light all around it. For a second it lay stunned, but then it began thrashing all the more fiercely. It was as though the beast sensed that its time was short; it tore at the vines that trapped it in a fury, ripping them away two or three at a time, its monstrous talons and unmeasurable strength making the task appear easy all of a sudden.

And then it was free.

To his left, Melanie recoiled as though struck physically and stumbled backwards, landing awkwardly on her backside. She did not move, her expression stunned and her eyes unfocused.

The Out-Dweller bellowed again, in victory Julian thought this time, from its tone, and pushed itself to its feet. It spun, turning its quartet of burning eyes onto Loran.

The Inquisitor stood tall - well, as tall as he was capable of - and met the Out-Dweller stare for stare. And all the while he kept up his chant, his words coming forth in the same steady rhythm but increasing in volume and power with each breath.

The Out-Dweller stepped toward Loran, but its movement was far slower than it had been just a moment ago. It looked at him for a second, perplexed, then its gaze went skyward and its eyes widened.

Above the beast, the wind, which now was whipping past Julian to rival any storm he had ever seen had gathered up all of the loose dust and debris in the area. A funnel formed just above the Out-Dweller, sort of an inverted tornado. All around the Out-Dweller, bits of grass lifted up, struggling against their roots to join the vortex above. More dust and loose dirt flew upward all around the beast.

Then, in the middle of the funnel came a flash of light, like a single star giving birth, directly above the Out-Dweller.

The beast howled then, its earlier cry of victory becoming one of desperate denial.

The Out-Dweller fell forward, hitting the ground with a near deafening THUMP, and then dug into the earth with its talons. It roared again, as though trying to call on its reserves of strength.

All around the beast, debris, small at first and then larger, began rushing toward the flickering light at the vortex's center. Watching them go, faster and faster, Julian was surprised that he was not following with them. But strong as the wind was, he felt no greater force than he had before.

And yet now things that were clearly large, nearly as large as he, were being pulled into that light.

Every time one of them struck the light, it flashed a bit brighter and expanded, casting a pure white illumination on the area.

One of the objects flew past his shoulder and Julian saw a black carapace and multitudes of long, clutching legs and pinchers that tried to grab him before it, too, was consumed by the light. And he understood. Everything that was being drawn into the vortex was something the Out-Dweller had brought over into this plane with it.

And after they were gone, the Out-Dweller would be next.

The Out-Dweller knew this as well. It bellowed again and tried to dig its feet into the ground, but its hooves could not dig as well as its talons and they gained no purchase. Again crying in denial, it was helpless to prevent its feet from being drawn upward. Finally, it sat there like a gymnast Julian saw in a traveling show once, standing upright on just the palms of his hands. But this time, the Out-Dweller was working to hold itself in place, its talons dug in deeply, desperately.

But still the vortex pulled it upwards.

Slowly, inexorably, one of the Out-Dweller's hands pulled free from the earth. For a second, Julian thought that would be it, but the beast flailed around and its talons came to rest on something else that was lying on the ground nearby. Something limp and bony, dressed in the robes of a mage.

Telurian.

The Out-Dweller drew the hapless mage closer to itself and

stared at him, its eyes filled with malevolent intent. Telurian jerked and then his eyes flew open, meeting the gaze of the Out-Dweller without any opportunity for defense.

Telurian's scream rang out, loud even above the howling tumult of the wind, the power of Loran's chant, and the rasping growl of the Out-Dweller's breathing. On and on the hapless mage screamed; though the Out-Dweller did nothing to him but hold him and look at him, it sounded as though he were being flayed alive, he screamed so. He began to spasm uncontrollably, his body flopping around like a puppet whose strings had been cut.

The Out-Dweller smiled slightly, a look of pure, evil enjoyment.

And then its other hand lost its grip on the earth, and the beast flew upwards into the vortex and the brilliant light at its center. The Out-Dweller struck the light, and it flared all the greater, lighting the area more intensely than the sun could have a noon.

And then the light was gone, and with it the storming wind and the struggling beast from the outer planes. Only Telurian remained. He seemed to hover in midair for several seconds, but then he fell to the ground.

The thud of his body landing seemed far louder than it should have in the absolute silence that followed.

❦ 35 ❦

FLOTSAM AND JETSAM

J ulian stood there, speechless. What could he say? His mind struggled to wrap itself around what had just happened, but it could not get there. He swallowed and tried a different tack. The Out-Dweller was gone. That much seemed certain.

That reality crept into his psyche, and all of a sudden relief flooded through him like a river past a dam that had been breeched. When he charged that thing with only his little dagger for a weapon, he truly had not though he would see the next hour, let alone the next ten minutes. And yet, here he stood, and the Out-Dweller had, apparently, been vanquished.

He was on his knees. When that happened, Julian could not say. But right then, it did not seem inappropriate.

"It worked." Melanie sounded just as relieved as he did, but when Julian turned his head to look at her, she was still on her feet. Showoff.

"Of course it worked." Loran sniffed contemptuously as he replied, then strolled, apparently without care as though he had just finished his early afternoon tea, over toward where Telurian lay. He stopped when he reached the other mage and looked down at him, frowning for a long moment before squatting down next to him.

Melanie crossed her arms under her breasts and stared at him, not at all pleased by his response. "You're welcome," she said, finally, no small amount of scorn in her tone.

Loran glanced at her and shook his head slightly, but did not reply. Telurian had his entire attention. Loran felt alongside the other mage's neck for his pulse, then forced his eyelid open. He peered into Telurian's eye for a long while, then sighed. He released the fallen mage and stood, wiping his fingers on his cloak as though he had dragged them through mud, his expression deeply saddened.

"Is he alive?" Raedrick asked. He had regained his footing and his equilibrium, and he stood facing Loran with his best all-business expression on his face.

Loran shrugged. "After a fashion."

"Meaning what?"

Loran turned a cool gaze on Raedrick and was silent for several seconds. Then he sighed and lowered his eyes to again look at Telurian's prone form. "His body lives. And will, if history carries out, accept food and water when forced to. But his essence...his mind..." Loran shook his head and grimaced. "We do not know whether he still lurks somewhere within his body, insanely driven to hide away from the world, or whether the Out-Dweller drew him out and bore him back into the netherworld with it."

Julian shuddered at the thought of going to wherever the Out-Dweller came from. It could only be horrid, being there. He flashed back to the feeling of the Out-Dweller's cronies crawling all over him, hurting him everywhere and depriving him even of breath even as they blotted out any shred of light and beauty. Horrid would not even begin to describe what it would be like to live where those things dwelled.

He cleared his throat. "Sounds like this has happened before."

Loran glanced Julian's way and nodded. "There are some

historical accounts, but none match what Telurian did. At least none within the last four centuries." He sighed. "I had thought...hoped...that he had only contacted a lesser being from the dark planes, and that he had bound the creature to his will, to do evil according to his whims."

"Didn't he?"

Loran shook his head in response to Raedrick's words. "Did you not see that creature? Did you not hear Telurian's words?" He gestured at the prone man, who was beginning to drool all over himself. "Telurian was far from the strongest man I ever taught, but even he could have dealt with one of the lesser Out-Dwellers. No," he shook his head again, "somehow he invited a Lord of the netherworld over, and very quickly *it* overwhelmed *him* and twisted him to its will." He lowered his eyes, sadly. "And now he has paid the price."

Loran was silent for a long moment. Then he drew in a deep breath, through his nostrils, and looked back up at Raedrick, then Julian. "I will need your help to get him back to town." His eyes held a question, nearly a pleading, and a deep sorrow that Julian would not have expected from a man who had been sent to hunt down a criminal.

Then Julian remembered that Loran said Telurian had studied beneath him at some point. Almost against his will, Julian found he could understand, even relate, to Loran's pain. He had helped train many young recruits who showed up to his unit, barely trained and completely unprepared for the realities of life along the battle lines. More of those young men - Julian refused to allow himself to admit that they were not really all that much younger than he was himself - died on the battlefield because he and his fellows did not have time to prepare them adequately than he liked to recall.

But he did recall the ache in his heart...in his soul...every time one of them passed, far too early and far too uselessly.

Julian nodded his assent. He would help carry Telurian's body - and it was just a body, little more than mobile flesh, if his mind truly had been sucked away by that beast - back to town. Much as he disliked Loran, he could not deny the bond the inquisitor felt for his former student, and Julian could not turn his back on that.

Melanie, however...

"What do you mean, he's paid the price?" Her tone was hot, the sort of hot that Julian had learned over the last several months of knowing her foretold that the person she was speaking to was treading on extremely - extremely- dangerous ground. "You're not going to just let him go on living, after what he did?"

Her words were met only be silence for a time. Julian thought about responding, to explain things, but found he did not have the words. He looked over at Raedrick and saw that his one-time squad leader was in a similar quandary; he understood the root of Loran's feelings, just as Julian did, and that emotion conflicted with his innate desire to see justice done.

And how could justice be done while Telurian breathed, when so many of his victims did not?

Finally, Loran answered. His tone was cold, and he looked at Melanie with the contempt one normally reserves for the lowliest of slaves. "I mean what I say, woman." He imparted the word "woman" with such scorn and derision that, for a moment, Julian thought he would perhaps vomit from having to voice such a word. Then he continued, in a more normal tone. Cold, but normal. "The torment he endures at the hands of the Out-Dweller far surpasses any that we mortals could inflict." He scowled slightly, then added, "But if perchance he somehow managed to escape that fate, and he comes back to his senses, he will stand trial and be punished according to the law."

With that, he turned his back on Melanie and once again squatted down next to Telurian.

"You believe he really was brought over with the beast." Raedrick was stating a fact, not asking a question.

Loran nodded, saying nothing more.

Raedrick returned the nod, his face solemn. The two men shared a long look. Then finally, Raedrick nodded again, and

Loran inclined his head, his lips turning upwards into a slight smile of gratitude. Raedrick took a moment to locate his blade. He sheathed it and walked over to Telurian's body. Then he and Loran together lifted the fallen mage, and they began the long trek back to town.

Julian stayed behind with Melanie for a time. She had not budged from the spot where she stood, watching the Inquisitor and the Constable walking away with their burden. It took Julian a minute or two to realize she was crying. Or at least tears were dripping from her eyes.

"Are you alright?"

Melanie sniffed. "That man killed dozens, or more. And *he* lets him live." She drew herself up and inhaled quickly, steeling her expression into something that resembled a statue. "Timon was guilty only of teaching me what I wanted to learn, and they tortured him to death for it." She turned her head and looked at Julian, her eyes tight with suppressed pain and anger. "Do you call that justice, Julian?"

She did not wait for his answer, but went stalking after the two men, and their burden.

Julian lingered for a time, watching them go.

He had no good answer to her question.

✵ 36 ✵

FAREWELLS

The grooms lifted Telurian into his saddle. The mage went along limply, almost sliding off the horse altogether before the two young men got him properly situated. They lingered for a few moments, watching him warily as though expecting him to slump over and fall off any second.

And small wonder. The mage just sat there, staring blankly at the area in front of himself, his face expressionless and his mouth hanging slightly open. A drop of drool slowly began to accumulate at the corner of his mouth, but he did not lift a hand to stop it. In fact, his hands never left his saddle horn; he had not even taken hold of the horse's reins.

If it were not for the dark blue robes, almost black, that he wore, and the golden necklace around his neck that announced his status as a member of the Magestirium, no one would take him for such a lofty personage.

But not so lofty any more.

Loran regarded the young grooms with a disapproving frown and waved them away. One of them opened his mouth to object, no doubt still concerned that Telurian would fall, but the look on Loran's face stopped him. The groom bobbed his head in a quick half-bow, then hurried away after his comrade, who had fled as soon as Loran indicated he should.

Julian did not watch them go. He stood beside Raedrick, across The Oarlock's stableyard from where Loran and his erstwhile fugitive were, and watched the Inquisitor's actions closely.

They were there to make sure Loran and Telurian left town quickly, and caused no more trouble as they did. And to make sure they avoided one particular bit of trouble more than any other.

Loran scowled after the grooms, then flung his saddlebags over his own horse's back. He cinching up his own robes before mounting - he had worn his formal attire for departure, and not just because he had met with the Mayor earlier in the morning to bid farewell. And so the Mayor could try to do some damage control.

Small chance of that.

Loran grabbed the reins of Telurian's horse and wrapped them around his own saddle horn, then made a soft clucking noise that just barely carried to Julian's ear. His horse began walking forward at a slow walk, and Loran nudged it to the left, toward the open gateway leading out to the street. As he turned, his eyes alighted on Julian and Raedrick, and his expression grew a bit more dark than it had been before.

Loran pulled his horse to a halt when he was a few paces away from them and nodded quickly, the short nod of superior to subordinate, one meant to remind the subordinate of his place.

"Constables. Here to see me off, I presume."

Raedrick returned the nod with one that was deep enough to convey respect but shallow enough to discount the difference in stature between them. "Just making sure you have all that you need."

Loran sniffed, and was silent for a moment. His eyes moved slowly from Raedrick to Julian and back, but aside from that his expression did not change.

"You do not trust that I will do as we agreed and leave

your...woman...alone." His tone was neutral, but his eyes flashed with anger, and scorn. He did not like this arrangement one bit. That was hardly surprising.

"I did not say that." Raedrick, too, kept his tone neutral.

Loran rolled his eyes quickly. "I am a man of my word." He nudged his horse, turning it away from Julian and Raedrick, toward the gate. Then he paused, looking back at them. "Were I you, I would reconsider my choice of friends. A woman driven to revenge, against people who have not wronged her, is not..."

Julian could not help it. He interrupted Loran's words, speaking hotly. "You killed her lover."

Loran shook his head. "I brought a man to justice who was guilty of crimes against the King and the Magestirium. That this Timon was her lover was unfortunate. For her. But there was no malice meant in it."

"How can you say that?"

Loran looked at Julian like he was daft. "This man you fought some months ago. Isenholf. Did you bear malice toward his family and friends when you sent him to the gallows?"

Julian felt the wind taken out of his sails by Loran's words, and he closed his mouth without replying. No, he did not think about Isenholf's family at all when he put him on the cart for Mangin City, where a Magistrate who was empowered to deal with Capital cases held court. He would have preferred to settle it all locally, but their judge was only commissioned to handle more mundane issues. Julian supposed the powers that be in the Kingdom decided towns as small as Lydelton would not have to deal with those offenses, or at least not often enough to warrant the extra cost of a higher Magistrate and his staff.

But that was neither here nor there. Loran was right. Julian had not thought at all about the people who would be sorry to see good old Theobald hanged. Although, he could not fathom there were that many who fit the bill. But there must have been *someone*.

Loran smiled, ever so slightly, seeing that he had scored a point. "You see? We are not as different as you would like to think,

Constable Hinderbrook." He returned his gaze to Raedrick. "Of course, at the time we did not know the full extent of Timon's crimes, or of Mistress Klemins' participation in them. Had we..." He paused, meaningfully, then said, "Good health to you, Constables." Then he turned his back and nudged his horse's flanks with his heels.

The steed set off at a walk, and Telurian's horse followed suit. A moment later, the two men were gone from view.

"Do you really believe he won't tell his people about Melanie?" Julian said.

Raedrick frowned and shook his head, but said nothing. His eyes tracked toward where Loran must have been, had he followed the most efficient course toward Main Street and then out of town.

"Me neither."

Melanie's shop was open, for a wonder. It felt to Julian as though it had been closed for months, with all that had happened. Strange to think it had only been a few days.

He pushed the door open and stepped within, then paused for a moment, inhaling the odor of some exotic incense and smiling. Melanie always knew how to keep a welcoming feel about her place, but she had never burned this particular incense before. Or at least, Julian did not recognize it. It smelled expensive, though.

Melanie was seated on a stool behind her counter. She wore a simple but elegant green dress that was embroidered with flowers and birds around the ends of the sleeves and about her neck. She was reading a small book, but she looked up as the door swung closed behind Julian.

Upon seeing him, she quirked an eyebrow upwards and smiled, ever so slightly. "Julian."

"Feeling better?"

She shrugged, the smile leaving her face as quickly as it came. "Not particularly."

He walked over to the counter. There were a few nicknacks in a small bin at the counter's end, and he rummaged through them for a short while, trying to figure the right way to say this.

Melanie looked at him askance, but said nothing.

Finally, Julian decided to just put it out there. "Loran left town a couple hours ago."

He expected a reaction, but an almost un-caring shrug was not it. "So I heard."

Julian looked at her more closely. Her expression was nonchalant, but that indifference did not make it to her eyes. They were slightly bloodshot, and the bottom of her nose slightly reddened, as though she had the sniffles. Five to one odds she had cried herself to sleep the night before, and again on waking this morning.

He was not stupid enough to say that to her face, of course.

"I more than halfway expected you to make a try for him before he left. Wasn't that your plan?"

She frowned and looked away from Julian, toward the case of remedies in the center of her shop. "He knew I was coming, or he must have. He would have made preparations, and he is more than my match in a stand-up fight." She inhaled through her nose - that sounded suspiciously like a sniffle - then turned back to him and smiled more broadly. But again the smile did not reach her eyes. "The point was to get even, not to kill myself."

Julian nodded understanding. Melanie was no fool. He had overstated things a bit; he had been far from halfway expecting her to attack Loran. More like a third-way, or a quarter. All the same, though, she had been practically bursting at the seems a few times over the course of the night before last. And if...

But she had not. That was the important part. Well, *an* important part.

The other part was much more difficult.

He drew a deep breath. "Loran knows where you are now."

Melanie nodded, the smile fading again. Her eyes widened ever so slightly, and she suddenly looked nervous.

"I don't believe he'll hold that information back from the Magestirium and neither does Raedrick. Maybe it would be best if..."

Melanie held up a silencing hand, looking beyond nervous toward frightened. "Don't."

"Melanie, I..."

"Don't send me away, Julian."

Looking at her, he saw an openness, a...vulnerability...that he had never seen in her before. The facade of supreme confidence bordering on arrogance, the sense of quiet strength coupled with worldliness and knowledge that she normally projected was gone. All that remained was a woman suddenly afraid of losing... Losing what?

She sniffed again, and blinked to stop upwelling tears, but she was not successful. "I've finally made a home here. It's been so long since..." She wiped her eyes and coughed out a half-laugh that rang with self-directed disgust. She drew herself up, drawing a deep breath. "I'm not going anywhere. So don't try to suggest I do anything different."

And she was back, just like that. The stare she directed at Julian was challenging, daring him to push the topic.

"They'll send someone for you. Maybe several someones. You know that."

She nodded.

"And us as well, for harboring you."

That made her flinch, but the challenging stare never wavered.

Julian looked her in the eye for a few seconds, and as usual could not stop admiration from welling up within him. And not just for her looks, which would normally be enough in and of themselves. He was not sure he could stay firm like this in the face of what she faced, especially having witnessed what the Magestirium was capable of with Timon.

No, he was certain he could not stand firm. He, and Raedrick as well, had fled the consequences of his actions in the Army, rather than stay and face the headsman's axe.

That admiration just got larger.

"Just wanted to make sure we were all clear on that."

Melanie smiled again, ever so slightly, then nodded.

Julian returned the nod, then walked over to the the door. He reached for the latch, but paused and looked back at her. "See you at The Oarlock later?"

Melanie smiled at him, and for the first time since he walked in it seemed the smile was genuine. "Wouldn't miss it."

Julian returned the smile with a grin of his own, then he opened the door and went out. There was a town to see to, after all.

MESSAGE FROM THE AUTHOR

Thank you for reading my book. I hope you enjoyed reading it as much as I enjoyed writing it.

Every review helps an author out, so whether you loved this book, hated it, or something in between, please take a minute to tell other readers what you thought. All of the online retailers make it very easy to do, and I would really appreciate it.

Feel free to come say hi at my website or on Gab. I always enjoy hearing from readers, especially since you all are, collectively, my boss.

I also have a weekly podcast, Story Time With Michael Kingswood, where I read stories and talk through some of the latest goings on in my world. I'd love to see you there.

Thanks again. My best to you and yours.

Warm Regards,
Michael Kingswood

MAILING LIST

If you enjoyed this book and would like word on new releases and special deals from Michael Kingswood, sign up for his newsletter on his website. Guaranteed to be spam-free, you can opt out at any time. And you can rest assured he will not share your information with anyone, for any reason.

https://michaelkingswood.com/newsletter-signup/

MEMBERSHIP

Michael would like to invite you to become a supporting member of his website. Similar in concept to Patreon, a few dollars a month will give you access to exclusive content, and help him to focus more of his time to writing fun and exciting stories for your enjoyment.

Sign up at his website:

https://www.michaelkingswood.com/membership/join/

ABOUT THE AUTHOR

Michael Kingswood is 20-year veteran of the US Navy submarine force and a lifelong fan of science fiction and fantasy literature. His work has appeared in numerous collections and anthologies, to include the Fiction River Anthology series from WMG publishing. He holds a bachelors degree in Mechanical Engineering as well as a Master of Engineering Management and a Master of Business Administration. He has four children and currently resides in San Diego.

Find Michael Kingswood online at:

www.michaelkingswood.com

www.facebook.com/michael.kingswood

twitter.com/michaelkingswd

MORE BOOKS BY MICHAEL KINGSWOOD

GLIMMER VALE CHRONICLES

Glimmer Vale

Out-Dweller

Tollard's Peak

Robbed Blind

The Falconer's Stairs

Glimmer Vale Omnibus Edition #1

STORIES FROM GLIMMER VALE

Legacy

Hidden Magic

Captive Hearts

Wedding Gifts

Lost Credit

THE PERICLES CONSPIRACY

Passing In The Night

The Pericles Conspiracy

DAWN OF ENLIGHTENMENT

Masters Of The Sun

NOVELLAS

What Lurks Between

The Necromancer's Lair

The Champion

Veritas Morte

STORY COLLECTIONS

Stories From The Great Challenge

Tales Of Adventure #1

Tales Of Adventure #2

Short Story 10-Pack

A Jar Of Mixed Treats

Short Mystery 10-Pack

Stories From Glimmer Vale, Volume 1

SHORT FICTION

Michael has also published a number of shorter works, links to which can be found on his website.